W9-DDK-187

WITHDRAWN

MAY 06 2013

PUBLIC LIBRARY

URVE TAMBERG

THE DARKEST CORNER OF THE WORLD

DCB

Copyright © 2012 Urve Tamberg
This edition copyright © 2012 Cormorant Books Inc.
This is a first edition.

No part of this publication may be reproduced, stored in a retrieval system
or transmitted, in any form or by any means, without the prior written consent
of the publisher or a licence from The Canadian Copyright Licensing Agency
(Access Copyright). For an Access Copyright licence,
visit www.accesscopyright.ca or call toll free 1.800.893.5777.

  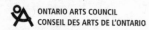

The publisher gratefully acknowledges the support of the Canada Council for the
Arts and the Ontario Arts Council for its publishing program. We acknowledge the
financial support of the Government of Canada through the Canada Book Fund
(CBF) for our publishing activities, and the Government of Ontario through the
Ontario Media Development Corporation, an agency of the Ontario Ministry of
Culture, and the Ontario Book Publishing Tax Credit Program.

LIBRARY AND ARCHIVES CANADA CATALOGUING IN PUBLICATION

Tamberg, Urve
The darkest corner of the world / Urve Tamberg.

Issued also in electronic formats.
ISBN 978-1-77086-214-2

1. World War, 1939–1945 — Estonia — Juvenile fiction.
I. Title.

PS8639.A557D37 2012   JC813'.6   C2012-903484-3

Cover photograph and design: Angel Guerra/Archetype
Interior text design: Tannice Goddard, Soul Oasis Networking
Printer: Trigraphik LBF

Printed and bound in Canada.

The interior of this book is printed on 100% post-consumer waste recycled paper.

DANCING CAT BOOKS
an imprint of Cormorant Books Inc.
390 Steelcase Road East, Markham, Ontario, L3R 1G2
www.cormorantbooks.com

To my parents,
Miralda and Leo,
who were generous, brave, and loving.

PART ONE

CHAPTER ONE

Tallinn, Estonia
June 1941

Madli yearned to eat the candy. Again her hand slipped into her skirt pocket. The wrapper crinkled. Inside was a delicious orange-flavoured hard sweet. The kind with a chewy centre. A year ago — a lifetime ago — she would've eaten two, maybe three in a row. She would've sucked until the hard candy coating dissolved, then sunk her teeth into the sticky sweetness.

Today, she'd toss the candy into the garbage.

Candy from Stalin.

At the special school assembly in the morning, recruiters for the Komsomol and Little Oktoberists had spewed propaganda to entice students to join the Communist party. Tomorrow, classmates would come with red scarves looped tight around their necks and take their place at the front of the class.

Like good comrades.

Like hell.

Not her. Not with Papa in jail and Kalju of age to be conscripted into the Soviet army.

In the last year, words like *arrest, deportation, jail,* and *torture*
slipped off people's lips every day. Words like *Britain, travel,* and
movie were rarely heard unless someone dared to reminisce about
the past, and then only at home in the quietest of whispers.

Tears brimmed and threatened to slide down her cheeks.
Madli blinked rapidly, as she adjusted her brown leather schoolbag across her chest. When would life be normal again?

Maybe, just maybe, life would be ordinary in the summer. In
a few days, after school ended, she and her brothers would leave
for her grandparents' farm on Hiiumaa Island. She brushed the
tears away.

Madli raced up the stone steps of Lühike Jalg and through the
long dark passageway that had connected the Upper and Lower
Town of Tallinn in medieval days. As she stepped onto Pikk
Jalg, the June sun blinded her. In the corner of her eye, a figure
loomed. Despite Madli's shuffle and sidestep, they collided with
a bone-jarring thud.

"Oh!" a strange voice said. A heavy parcel hit the ground. "Oh,
no."

Madli squinted. A girl stood on the sidewalk, empty handed,
mouth open, dark eyes wide. Thin, as everyone was these days,
and dressed in a flower-print blouse and plain blue skirt. A bit
older than Madli. Sixteen or seventeen. At first glance she seemed
familiar, but Madli focused on the white box labelled *Alpertson
Candy* on the ground beside her feet. Worry churned in Madli's
stomach. What if she insisted on payment for the damage? Their
money in the bank had been seized by the Soviets and Russian
rubles had replaced Estonian *kroons.*

"*Tuhat vabandust,*" Madli said, apologizing to the girl in
Estonian. Her schoolgirl Russian was adequate, but she refused

to speak it unless absolutely necessary. "I should've been watching where I was going." Her finger flew to her mouth and she gnawed the side of the nail.

"It's not your fault," the girl replied, also in fluent Estonian. Kind brown eyes examined Madli. "I was lost in thought and didn't see you." She continued to stare. "Don't you recognize me, Madli?"

Madli tried to focus even though her pulse still galloped. The girl looked familiar, but from where?

"Piano. Your lesson was after mine. Remember Madame Prideaux?" Imitating the teacher, the girl wagged her finger in mock earnestness. "It seems like ten years ago, not one."

The vision of Madame Prideaux with her scarlet, manicured nails clutching a ruler, tapping out rhythm made Madli's lips twitch. She mimicked the gesture as she examined the girl.

"Sarah." In the past year, Sarah's face had grown gaunt and her bony shoulders now poked through her blouse. Madli hoped only her appearance had changed and not her politics. These days, neighbours turned in neighbours for ridiculous reasons to gain favour with the Soviets. Communism was a contagion, passed quickly from person to person

The lump in Madli's stomach softened. "I'm so glad you're all right. What's in the box? Is anything broken?"

Sarah kneeled down and opened the lid. Colour exploded out of the box. She picked up one of the objects and gave it to Madli.

A tiny perfect strawberry rested in the palm of Madli's hand. It appeared so real she was tempted to pick off the leaves and pop it into her mouth, sure its juices would dribble down her chin. "Is it made of marzipan?"

"Yes." Sarah nodded and her dark curls bounced. "I'm delivering them to one of our customers."

Madli kneeled down and peered into the box. "They're works

of art." Exquisite marzipan fruit nestled together in the box. Velvet peaches, gleaming red apples, shiny limes, radiant oranges, and even bananas. "Nothing broken." Relief coursed through her. It could have been much worse. "Who are they for?"

"These are decorations for a Soviet officer's wedding celebration," Sarah replied.

Madli's shoulders relaxed. "I'm sorry I made you late." Sarah seemed unchanged despite the many months of Soviet occupation. "Are you still taking piano?"

"*Ostanovites!*" a deep voice boomed out in Russian. Boots pounded on the pavement behind her.

Madli's heart jumped into her throat. Instinct begged her to run, but common sense insisted she turn around. Two soldiers strode toward them with rifles slung over their shoulders. Khaki uniform shirts hung on their lanky frames.

Would they be arrested? And for what? The Soviet army never needed a good reason. Countless people had been killed or deported. Picked off like apples from a tree.

Her hands clenched. As if she could fight the Soviet army. Out of the corner of her eye, she noticed Sarah tug the charm on her necklace to the back so only the chain was visible. Madli touched the empty collar of her blouse, wishing for a second that she were flaunting a red Komsomol scarf. She lowered her eyes.

The dusty boots halted a couple of steps away. "Why are you loitering?"

Sarah answered the soldiers in fluent Russian. "I dropped the box by accident and she kindly stopped to help me."

The warmth in Sarah's voice made Madli's legs quiver. Had she been wrong about Sarah's allegiance? These days everyone lied — for a piece of bread, to keep their jobs, to keep their families safe. Anything to avoid being noticed by beady-eyed Soviet soldiers.

"And what do you say?" the voice asked.

Madli had to meet his gaze. She raised her eyes to see a vaguely good-looking young soldier staring at her. His dark-lashed hazel eyes were more curious than aggressive. Full lips eased into the tiniest of smiles. She took a deep breath and regretted it immediately. Stale cigarettes and sweat. She resisted wrinkling her nose. Rudeness might get her arrested.

"Aren't you special," he said. "Are those eyes real?" His fingers tugged unruly brown hair off his forehead.

One sky blue eye and one chocolate brown eye. She'd answered all the questions before. Yes, they were real. No, she was not a witch. Yes, she could see equally well with both. "*Da*," she said.

Madli glanced at the other soldier. Pimples covered his face and extended down his neck, disappearing into a grimy uniform shirt. Did these two even need to shave yet?

Messy Hair leaned closer. "You're lucky to be so memorable."

Madli held her tongue and her breath. Being memorable to the Soviet army was the last thing she wanted. Being unremarkable, being anonymous, being able to hide in plain sight — that would keep you alive. If you were memorable, they could find you. Arrest you. Kill you.

Messy Hair turned back to Sarah and butted the candy box with his rifle. "Open the box."

She lifted the lid and both soldiers peered inside. Pimple Neck grabbed an apple, inspected it, then threw it to the ground and crushed it under his boot. Messy Hair snatched a lime and did the same. They bent down to examine the flattened candy. "What are these?"

"Marzipan fruit for Comrade Kozlov's wedding," Sarah replied with a sweet smile. She tossed her dark curls and tilted her head.

Madli stared. Was Sarah actually flirting with the soldiers?

"What is marzipan?" Pimple Neck asked in a menacing tone.

A nervous giggle bubbled up. Madli quickly swallowed it. These Soviet soldiers didn't recognize marzipan. Did they consider it dangerous?

"Marzipan is a paste made of almonds and sugar," Sarah explained. "Would you care to try one?"

There was no mistaking her friendliness. The confident angle of her shoulders, her relaxed smile, the way she leaned toward the soldiers.

Messy Hair scanned Sarah to gauge her sincerity. He turned to Madli. An eyebrow rose to challenge Madli to break a smile or toss her hair.

Not her.

She folded her arms across her chest.

"We have more important things to do than talk to Estonian girls," Pimple Neck said. He thumped his comrade on the arm. "Let's go."

Messy Hair snorted with laughter. "*Da.*"

Neither girl moved until the soldiers rounded the corner. Madli exhaled slowly. "What did they think was in the box? It's just candy." She plucked her blouse away from her damp body.

Sarah shrugged and shut the lid. "Who knows? They don't need a reason to be suspicious. They have rifles." The afternoon sun emphasized the hollows in her face as she smiled. "I'm glad I didn't face the soldiers alone."

"You were so friendly with them." Madli was unsure if she wanted to hear Sarah's explanation.

"My mother says you can catch more flies with honey than with vinegar." Sarah grinned. "Even Soviet flies."

Flies should be swatted.

Sarah glanced at her watch. "Now I really am late." She smiled again. "It was good to see you again, Madli. *Nägemist!*"

"*Nägemist*, Sarah," Madli said. As she watched Sarah continue down the ancient cobblestone road, a twinge of sadness made her throat swell. Life had been so different before the occupation. Last June hundreds of Soviet tanks and Jeeps had thundered into the streets of Tallinn, and Red Army soldiers had swarmed the city. The scarlet Soviet hammer and sickle replaced the blue, black, and white Estonian flag. A few days later, she had thrown out her favourite red sweater.

The rest of the way home Madli clutched her schoolbag like a shield as she resisted the urge to peer around every corner.

Madli plodded up the dingy stairwell leading to their small second-floor apartment in the old part of town. Fingerprints and long scratches covered the grey walls. Her finger traced the black gouge snaking above the banister. It had been caused by the piano, or maybe the armoire Papa had commissioned as a wedding gift. Mama couldn't bear to leave either behind when they were forced to move out of their house by the Red Army.

Inside the apartment, the scent of last night's cabbage dinner lingered in the air. Madli breathed through her mouth. She hated this place and longed for their real home, with its garden filled with lilacs in the spring, its yard with the gnarled old apple tree she had climbed playing hide-and-seek. In their house, cabbage smells had been swept away by the fresh air that blew through large windows.

"*Tere*," Madli greeted as she dropped her bag by the door beside the other two schoolbags. Kalju and Peeter were already home. Mama insisted either Kalju or Madli walk Peeter home from school every day. As if a nineteen-year-old boy or fifteen-year-old girl could protect a seven-year-old from the Soviet army.

A flicker of worry shot through her: Mama was late getting home from work. Fearing the worst was normal. As Madli headed toward the kitchen, she tripped over one of Kalju's shoes. *"Kurat,"* she cursed under her breath, kicking it toward the wall. "Nine square metres per person. They treat us like we're cattle in a barn!"

"What?" Peeter asked from the bedroom.

"Nothing." Madli retrieved the shoe. The new Soviet law forbade people from living in homes that had more than nine square metres per person, and their new apartment was so small she was surprised Peeter couldn't hear her thoughts. She bent down to place the shoe along the wall. At least they didn't share their apartment with another family.

Madli continued to the kitchen to prepare dinner. Her hand trembled as she peeled the first potato. Soon the everyday rhythm calmed her nerves. She was peeling and slicing when footsteps headed toward her.

Kalju rummaged through the bread box. "What's for dinner?" came out as "Waas fur dinne?" with a mouthful of black bread. He chewed. "Wait, I know. Potatoes and more potatoes." He grabbed another slice of bread.

Madli nodded. Her brother could inhale food the way most people inhaled air, but the recent shortages meant his shirt hung loosely from his thin shoulders and his pants — definitely shorter than at Christmas — skimmed the laces of his shoes.

"And some salted herring," she said. Where was Mama?

"I'm going to do my assignment." He headed back toward the living room. "Our chemistry professor is evil."

"Mama should be home any minute." Madli filled a pot with water and lit the gas stove. She pulled five plates out of the cupboard then slid one back. Wishful thinking wouldn't bring Papa back.

A few minutes later, Mama rushed in the door, calling "Kalju, Madli, Peeter," as if she were taking inventory. From the bedroom came a couple of grunts in response.

A familiar hint of antiseptic and soap accompanied Mama into the kitchen.

"How was work?" Madli kissed Mama's cheek. The summer sun had left a glow on her mother's face.

"I had to stay late today." Mama peered into the pot. "A woman brought in a prescription for a special cream and it took time to prepare. Dinner almost done?"

Madli nodded. "Boys! Come eat!" she called.

Mama embraced both boys in a hug, but lingered with her arms around her youngest son, resting her chin on Peeter's downy blond head. Since Papa had been arrested Mama smothered them with affection.

At the table, Kalju buried his nose in his food, scooping it into his mouth. Peeter devoured the potatoes but picked at his fish. Mama slid a few pieces of herring onto Kalju's plate.

After everyone had eaten, Madli told them about Sarah. "I was so relieved to see a familiar face."

"I remember her." Mama wiped her mouth with a napkin. "Sarah Goldberg. Nice girl. Jewish."

The image of Sarah flicking the charm on her necklace returned to Madli. "Of course. Her Star of David necklace. She tucked it behind her when the soldiers came."

"What soldiers?" Mama asked quickly.

"Nothing happened," Madli said. She shouldn't have mentioned them. Mama worried so much. "They wandered by as Sarah and I talked."

Mama's eyes narrowed but she didn't press the issue.

"Bloody Soviets!" Kalju cursed. "Give them a rifle and they'd stop you if you were combing your hair on the street."

Mama gave him a glare to tell him to mind what he said in front of Peeter.

"We're sitting here like puppets, waiting for our strings to be pulled." Kalju mimicked a puppeteer.

"It could be worse." Mama twitched her eyebrows at Kalju as she got up and filled the sink to wash the dishes.

"I'll clear the table." Madli shot her own stare at Kalju. No one could fight the Soviets. The entire population of Estonia seemed about the size of one Russian family. Papa had been confident it would be a matter of time before the Americans or British rescued them. This time he'd been wrong.

"How could things be worse?" A frown clouded Peeter's face. "I can't even have candy!" His lower lip quivered.

Madli clattered the plates, knives, and forks together to make as much noise as possible. She hadn't mentioned the recruitment tactics at school. If Peeter started talking about the Little Oktoberists both Mama and Kalju would erupt.

"We had to move to a teeny tiny apartment. There's no more Christmas or Easter. What's good about that?" Tears spattered on the front of Peeter's white shirt.

Mama stood with her arms covered in soapy lather.

Madli caught her eye, placed the plates on the counter and scooted Peeter off the chair and into her lap. "Don't worry, we'll be safe," she said automatically.

Peeter cried harder. "Liar! Papa wasn't safe."

Madli hugged Peeter tight as she swayed back and forth. When the Communists had arrested Papa at the end of November, she'd assumed they were crazy. What kind of threat was a history professor? Now she knew his words had been considered treasonous by the Soviet regime. His unpublished manuscript about the history of Estonia lay in her underwear drawer; it included details from the secret clause of the Molotov-Ribbentrop Pact. Many people suspected that the Nazis and Soviets had signed more than an economic agreement and non-aggression pact in August 1939: Papa wanted to the world to know that, in exchange for Germany and the Soviet Union not attacking each other, eastern Europe had been divided into spheres of influence. Like pawns in a chess game. The Soviet Union got the Baltics, Finland, and eastern Poland. Germany got the rest of of Poland, which it had attacked on September 1, 1939, starting World War II. The Soviets didn't know about the manuscript, but they knew about his opinions.

If anyone found out she had this information, the whole family would be arrested.

Or worse.

"We're not going to fall apart," Mama said. "Papa wouldn't want that. He can take care of himself. He fought in the War of Independence when he was sixteen. He's smarter than a million Red Army soldiers."

Kalju snorted. "Not even a cat is safe. Mrs. Valge's neighbours complained about her cat, and the next thing she was gone. So was the cat. The powerful Red Army deported a cat." Kalju folded his arms across his chest.

"Kalju! That's enough!" Mama swung around. Soap dripped onto the floor from her lathered hands. "Papa needs us to be strong." She turned to finish the dishes. Seconds passed before the clatter of dishes filled the room.

"I liked our old life better." Peeter choked back sobs.

Who didn't? Madli continued to sway with him as she remembered movies from Europe and America. *Tarzan* with Johnny Weissmuller was her favourite. She'd seen it three times with her best friend, Helga. The two of them practised the Tarzan yell until Mama shooed them out of the house with a broom.

Papa had taken her to Paris before the war. She'd drunk the best hot chocolate in the world while sitting in a tiny cafe on Boulevard Saint-Germain. At the top of the Eiffel Tower she'd huddled with Papa when the storm clouds rolled in across the city. Papa bought her the navy blue coat with fox collar and cuffs. Far too small now. This winter she'd wear Mama's old coat again.

Helga and her family had been called back to Germany by Hitler in October. Making new friends was impossible. No one wanted to associate with a family possibly targeted for arrest.

Madli wiped Peeter's nose with her napkin. "Don't say that." She forced enthusiasm into her voice. "I can't wait for summer vacation. Four more sleeps 'til we go to Hiiumaa."

Peeter's tension melted at the mention of summer vacation.

"Why don't you pack your clothes for the trip?" Madli nudged him to stand.

Peeter drew his sleeve across his nose. "All right." He shuffled to the bedroom.

"A summer at Grandpa's farm will be good for him," Mama said. "Good for all of you." She plunged her hands into the soapy water. "Away from this."

Madli grabbed a dish towel. Away from the ever-present soldiers in the street. Away from this dingy apartment. Away from Papa.

Each week Mama took leftover food and a letter from them to Patarei prison and handed it to the guard. Mama hadn't seen Papa, but figured that as long as they accepted packages for him he was alive. Kalju once whispered to Madli that this didn't mean anything, only that the guards took the food for themselves.

As Madli finished drying the dishes, the phone rang. "I'll get it." She dropped her towel on the counter and went into the living room. "Hello?"

"Is your mother there?" a male voice asked.

"Uncle Jüri?"

"Your aunt Erika has broken her leg." His voice cracked as he spoke.

"*Kui hirmus!*" Madli exclaimed, only mildly surprised. Aunt

Erika was three times the size of Mama and tripped over the smallest things. It was hard to believe they were sisters.

"Mama!" she hollered. "Come quick. It's Uncle Jüri."

Mama came and snatched the receiver from Madli. "How awful. What happened? How is she?" Mama fired questions at Uncle Jüri.

Based on her short silences, she was getting his usual compact answers.

"Yes, I can come." She jammed the receiver back into place. Wrinkles etched Mama's forehead. "Poor Erika. She'll have a cast on for weeks. Uncle Jüri is useless in the kitchen and worse with sick people." She twisted her apron into a spiral. "This is as unexpected as a bang from a broom handle." Mama smoothed the apron out. "I'm going to pack my clothes and stay with them. Uncle Jüri is on his way to pick me up."

Mama's damp hands cupped Madli's face. "Sorry, *kalli*. I can count on you. Kalju will help."

Madli nodded. Kalju would give orders. Since Papa's arrest, he attempted to be the man of the family. Mostly, that consisted of telling her to do things she was going to do anyway.

"Don't worry." She couldn't show Mama her confidence had been rattled by the soldiers. Had she bumped into Sarah minutes earlier or later, nothing would have happened. Had Papa not worked late that night ... The randomness of events tormented her with equal doses of hope and despair.

Mama kissed Madli's forehead. "It's for a few days until you go to Hiiumaa. I'll call you every day. Uncle Jüri will pick you up Sunday at noon as planned and bring you to Aunt Erika's so we'll be together for a night before you leave."

Madli nodded.

If only Aunt Erika had fallen next week when she'd be in Hiiumaa.

CHAPTER TWO

After Mama left and the boys settled in the living room for a game of cards, Madli escaped to the bedroom she shared with Kalju and Peeter and the monstrous armoire. Through the open window, the conversation from the upstairs apartment floated down. Light footsteps back and forth meant the two little boys were preparing for bed. Trains rumbled slowly along the tracks, cars clanging together as the procession stopped and started.

Madli scrambled into her nightgown, then draped her clothes over a wooden chair between the beds. The same outfit would do for tomorrow. They no longer had a servant to wash and clean.

The candy fell to the floor.

Madli stared at it. Who'd know if she ate it? It didn't mean she'd suddenly sprout a red neckerchief and salute the sickle and hammer. It was only a candy. She picked it up and unwrapped it. The tip of her tongue licked the sweetness. Somehow the candy ended up in her mouth. Wonderful, delicious, orangey bliss. It would be wasteful to spit it out.

Guilt throbbed, first in her mind then in her heart. She walked over to the window. Phffft. The candy flew through the air. The taste remained on her tongue, taunting her.

On the bed, Madli settled onto her stomach and pulled out her diary from underneath the pillow. When Papa returned, she wanted to tell him everything. About the secret Christmas celebration they'd had with small candles lit, curtains closed, and the scent of pine boughs. About this horrible, tiny apartment they'd moved to in February. He'd laugh about her beating Kalju at chess six times in a row. She'd confide in him about the candy. He'd be proud of her for spitting it out.

The diary fell open at the first entry.

Tuesday, November 12, 1940
Papa didn't come home tonight.

Reading the sentence always made her throat thicken and the pencil in her hand tremble. That night it had taken all her energy to write those words. Tears had blinded her and dripped onto the diary, leaving the paper puckered. Each time she opened the diary, it fell open at the first page and she had to read that sentence. Like rubbing salt in a wound.

I'm sure the arrest is a terrible mistake. He's a history professor, not a spy.

But the Soviets didn't agree with Estonia's version of history. Lies, they called it. Papa called it the truth. As a world renowned history scholar, he wanted to bring attention to the reality of the Soviet occupation. The puppet government put in place during the summer of 1940. The arrests. The terror. He'd secretly finished his manuscript and was planning to smuggle it to his publisher in London.

Shortly after his arrest, the Soviets burned books that didn't fit their version of the truth. Bibles, history books, novels, English literature. Anything that wouldn't make people better comrades.

Thursday, June 12, 1941

Kallis Papa,

School is almost over. We're leaving in a few days to spend the whole summer at Grandpa and Nana's farm. Eight weeks away from Tallinn. Eight weeks without soldiers at every corner. Eight weeks is forever. Maybe the Soviets will be gone by the time we get back.

Don't worry — I'll take your manuscript with me to Hiiumaa. I'll hide it and keep it safe for you. No one knows I have the papers. Not Mama, not Kalju, and certainly not Peeter. When you come home, you'll be so proud of me.

I think about our stupid argument the night before your arrest. How I wouldn't speak to you the next day. I'll never forgive myself if something happens. That night can't be my last memory of you.

I'll make you proud.

Cards slapped on the table and a whoop came from Kalju. Their game was over. Madli slid the diary back under the pillow. She'd write later. This time of year, the sun barely skimmed the horizon and enough light came through the window even at midnight.

Her brothers invaded the small bedroom and organized themselves for the night.

"I can't wait to take the boat to Hiiumaa." Peeter climbed into bed. "Madli, how many more days?"

"Four more sleeps." Lavender grey sky filled the window. She missed seeing the stars in the summer.

"Grandpa and Nana will have lots of milk for my porridge and butter for my bread," Peeter said.

"I know you can't wait." Kalju tucked himself into bed. "To see your friends."

Madli caught the sly tease in his voice and ignored it. "Wild strawberries everywhere. I'm going to eat them until my fingertips turn red."

"I hear Toomas enjoys strawberries as well." Kalju drew out the vowels in his name.

Heat rose to her cheeks and she burrowed deeper under the covers. At the end of last summer the entire village had gathered to celebrate a wedding. As the accordion and fiddler tried to outdo each other in a toe-tapping polka, she had swirled her skirt to the beat of the music. From across the dance floor, Toomas had caught her eye and sauntered toward her with an impossible-to-resist grin. Her heart had started to pound. It raced a little faster as he tilted his head toward the dance floor and caught her hand. Warm callused fingers enveloped hers and her heart actually skipped a beat. Face to face, her eyes locked with his. Madli placed her hands on his solid shoulders. She nearly fainted when his hands wrapped around her waist. Slowly, they began to polka, but soon her feet skimmed the ground as they spun faster and faster. The rest of the night they danced until exhaustion forced them to collapse under the trees. Two days later, he came to the harbour to wave goodbye as the ferry left for the mainland.

"And Nana's delicious pancakes," Madli hoped conversation about food would distract Kalju. If he knew Toomas was constantly in her thoughts, he'd tease her mercilessly. In a few days, she and Toomas would dance until dawn at the Midsummer party. She'd try not to giggle at his silly jokes. Perhaps they'd search for the mythical blooming fern. Jaanipäev was a night when magic could happen. Legend had it that at midnight the fern would start to bloom. Those who found it would be able to achieve anything they wanted. Countless couples had wandered into the forest, though no fern blossoms had ever been found.

"I'm so hungry I'll eat the grass." Kalju stretched his length along the mattress. "You'll find me grazing beside the cows."

Madli's imagination switched to a picture of her tall, lanky brother on his hands and knees amongst a herd of cattle. "Milk and grass. What could be better? Those cows better look out for you. You'll wrestle them away from the clover."

Kalju mooed.

They giggled.

"Will we build a huge bonfire again?" Peeter asked. "Will they burn the boats on the sea? They can't stop Midsummer, can they?"

"It's not a religious celebration, so how could the Soviets object to it?" Madli replied, though she knew they could object to anything.

"We need to build the biggest bonfire in the world," Peeter said. "The bigger it is, the more it'll protect against evil spirits."

"It's not the evil spirits I'm worried about this year," Kalju said. "It's the evil people. A bonfire won't protect us. What we really need are weapons — guns, rifles, knives." His voice got louder.

"We could use a little magic, couldn't we?" Madli interrupted Kalju's tirade. "Peeter, do you know the story about Lake Ülemiste?"

"I don't remember," Peeter said.

"I'll tell you the story if you promise to go right to sleep," she said.

"All right," Peeter said. "Is it a scary story? I like scary stories now."

"It's only scary if it comes true. The legend is that the grey old man who lives in Lake Ülemiste comes out each Midsummer night's eve to ask whether the town of Tallinn has been completed."

"Tallinn has been here for hundreds of years so it must be finished," Peeter said.

"According to the legend if the town is ready, he'll release the waters of the lake and drown the town. That's why he's always been told the town is not completed yet," Madli said. "And now it's time for sleep. Goodnight." She pulled the covers up, rolled over and closed her eyes.

"If I see that grey old man this year, I'm going to tell him that Tallinn is finished," Kalju said. "I'm pretty sure those Soviet soldiers can't swim."

The next day was the last day of school. As Madli and Peeter walked home, Peeter hopped from cobblestone to cobblestone to avoid the cracks. "Madli, do you think anything bad will happen to us because it's Friday the thirteenth?"

"Only if you join the Little Oktoberists." She zigged and zagged after him. "Kalju and I will be your personal bad luck."

Peeter stopped. "I want to eat candy and play games with my new friends." His voice came out quiet and serious. "If they join, they'll sit at the front of the class. I'll sit in the very last row!" His brows drew together in a frown.

Madli bent down so her eyes were level with his. She snatched his hand and squeezed it tight. "It should take a lot more than candy to want to join the Communist party."

"Don't hurt me." Peeter pulled his hand away and crossed his arms. "They said everyone should join." His voice rose. "We're all comrades."

"Shhh," Madli hissed. "If they make us join, we'll be radish Communists."

Peeter wrinkled his forehead. "We'll eat radishes instead of candy? Yuck!"

"No." She managed a grin. "It's a joke. What is red on the outside and white on the inside?"

Peeter shook his head.

"A radish Communist. Someone who pretends to be a Soviet Communist, but really, in their heart, is true to Estonia." Madli didn't add that this would be to avoid being thrown in jail or killed by the Red Army.

The furrow between his brows deepened. "I thought lying was bad."

"The Soviets are in power and they outnumber us. By a lot," Madli said. "We can't fight them so we lie to protect ourselves."

"Oh." Peeter's face smoothed out. "We pretend."

"Exactly. We pretend."

"Then why can't I pretend to join?" Peeter stuck out his tongue. He scooted down the road.

Silly boy. Madli sped up to chase him. A small object gleamed between the cobblestones at the side of the road. She jogged over to pick it up. "Wait. I found something."

"What is it?" Peeter asked.

"It's an Estonian *kroon*," Madli said. "Absolutely worthless." She held it out to Peeter. "I'm tempted to leave it on the road, but I'll keep it. Perhaps it'll bring me luck."

"You can use it when Estonia is free," Peeter said.

Madli shrugged her shoulders, but slipped it into her pocket as they continued home.

The phone was ringing as Madli opened the apartment door.

"Hello, Madli." Mama's voice sounded tinny and faint.

"How's Aunt Erika?"

"They've set her leg in a cast," Mama said in a breathless voice. "She's absolutely miserable. Her leg hurts. Props it up with a pillow. Takes the pillow away five minutes later. She's always hungry." Silence. "I'll stay here for a while," Mama said in a more normal voice. "They'll cover for me at work, thank goodness. Can you bring me a few things on Sunday? Write them down so you won't forget." She listed the items. "And one more thing. Can you go by the pharmacy tomorrow? I'll call them. Aunt Erika's medicine will be waiting for you."

"Are you all right, Mama?" Madli asked.

"Of course, *kalli*," Mama said. "Can you help the boys pack for Hiiumaa?" More silence. "If Kalju's shirts are too small for him, Papa's clothes are in his suitcase in the hall closet. He won't mind lending them to Kalju."

Madli's eyes blurred. When they moved into the apartment, Madli had been so relieved that Mama had finally packed up Papa's clothes and toiletries. At their house, Madli had brushed her teeth with closed eyes so she wouldn't notice his toothbrush and razor beside the sink in the bathroom.

"Bye, Mama," Madli whispered.

After dinner Madli pulled out her suitcase and opened the door of her closet. Not much choice. With a sigh, she pulled out five hideous summer dresses with their hems let down as far as they would go. Behind them hung her navy blue wool coat. She ran her hand over the fox collar, then found a bathing suit that barely fit, underwear and socks, nightgowns, three sweaters (two were Mama's old ones), a couple of skirts and blouses, a coat, a pair of shoes and sandals, and Liisu, her doll. What she wouldn't give for a new dress for the Midsummer party. Preferably in her favourite shade of cornflower blue. It would have a thin belt to accentuate her slender waist. New white leather sandals would complete the outfit.

She gave a small stack of books on Marxist-Leninist theory a deft kick, and they landed in the back of the closet.

Madli rummaged beneath her underwear in the second drawer of the bureau and pulled out a sheaf of papers bound with twine. Papa's manuscript. She hugged it close and took comfort from the papery smell. A faint whiff of cigar wafted up. She inhaled each last molecule.

Madli tucked the papers into the bottom of the suitcase. When she finished packing, she placed her folded travel clothes on top of the case and her shoes beside it. Ready to go.

She helped Peeter pack as Kalju stuffed his clothes into Papa's old black leather suitcase. She fell asleep dreaming of eating wild strawberries with Toomas.

CHAPTER THREE

A strange noise from upstairs woke her. Madli scanned the ceiling as if to bore a hole through the wood with her eyes. It was past two o'clock in the morning. What were the upstairs neighbours doing at this time of night? Heavy footsteps pounded overhead and her heart began to hammer. Those footsteps didn't belong to the family.

Madli knew the family's steps as well as she knew her own: Mr. Kiik strode across the room; Mrs. Kiik tread lightly and padded back and forth numerous times; the children, two boys younger than Peeter, jumped and skipped.

Tonight men stomped in heavy boots.

A door slammed shut. Loud male voices commanded.

Madli's heart thumped faster and faster until she could barely hear.

"What's happening?" Peeter slurred his words, half asleep.

Madli slid out of bed and knelt beside him. "Shhhh. Nothing is happening." Her voice quivered, but he was too sleepy to notice. Her shaky hand stroked his back until his face relaxed into innocent sleep. "Back to sleep. It's all fine." She smoothed the covers over him. It's all fine, she told herself.

A heavy object dragged across the floor. More yelling.

Rushing blood filled Madli's ears. What was going on upstairs? On her hands and knees, she crawled to the window, hovered at the corner, then peered over the windowsill. Her eyes scoured the stillness outside at the back of the building. She sank to the floor under the window and strained to hear more. On this warm summer night, the Kiiks had probably left their window open as well.

"Hurry up," a deep voice commanded in Russian. "We don't have all night to wait while you pack."

Why would they be packing in the middle of the night? Where were they going? Dizziness swirled. She'd forgotten to breathe. A few deep breaths tamed the terror.

Lighter footsteps scrambled back and forth across the upstairs floor. Mrs. Kiik would be packing. Muffled crying filtered through the night air.

"What's going on?" Kalju asked in a gravelly sleep-filled voice. He got out of bed and strolled over to the window. "Why are you on the floor?" He peered out between the flimsy curtains.

Madli grabbed his nightshirt and pulled him down. "Shhh! Something is happening."

Peeter grunted, threw an arm over his head, then settled back to sleep. Thank goodness he was a deep sleeper.

With Kalju awake, she focused on the noises upstairs and less on her panic. Boots thumped on the ceiling then faded away. They were leaving the bedroom and moving to the living room.

"What's ...?" Kalju said.

"Shhhhhh!" Madli put a finger to her lips.

Kalju's eyes widened as he heard men shout in Russian.

"Let's go to the living room," Madli said. All the apartments were identical in layout.

Kalju crawled into the hallway and she followed. As she passed the closet, she pulled out her tennis racquet. In the living room, like a moth drawn to light, she edged over to the window and peered out onto the corner. A streetlight cast shadows over the silent street. In the middle of their quiet road, a large truck was parked outside the apartment building. At least a dozen people stood in the open back of the truck. Why were people crowding onto a truck in the middle of the night? Where could they be going? Two men with rifles paced casually on the sidewalk. The unmistakable peaked cap of the Soviet army uniform topped their heads.

Kalju kneeled at the other end of the window. Even from a distance, the heat of his rage made the hairs on her arms stand up. Madli sat down under the window, hugged her knees and strained her ears to hear every step, every word, every terrifying sound. Nausea crawled into her throat and wove its way to her stomach. Furniture scraped against the floor and drawers slammed shut. Each time she heard a new noise she twitched like a dry leaf in autumn.

Silence.

Madli stopped breathing. She stopped moving, but she couldn't stop her heart from pounding. It hadn't occurred to her the soldiers might come for them as well.

There was no escape.

Would they knock or would they just charge in? She almost snorted with laughter. Why would the Red Army knock? To be polite?

She took a deep breath, laid her palms on the floor, tried to keep the world from spinning. Hysteria could get them killed.

More laughter threatened. Of course, doing nothing would get them killed too.

"I'm not going like a sheep to slaughter," Kalju said quietly.

The way Papa did. Kalju didn't dare speak those words, but she knew he was angry at Papa for not fighting back. She'd seen the police escort him out of the building. Kalju hadn't. He didn't understand. She clutched her tennis racquet.

Heavy footsteps clomped down the stairs and past their apartment. The noise faded onto the street.

Like a jellyfish thrown from the sea she lay motionless. She had to find out what was happening to the Kiiks. She compelled her brain to send signals to her legs and arms. A few seconds of studied effort later, she peeked again at the corner. The Kiiks stood on the sidewalk with suitcases and bags. They appeared bulky and fat, dressed in heavy coats despite the warmth of the summer night.

Two guards shadowed them with rifles at the ready and hustled them into the back of the truck. There didn't appear to be enough room, but the shadows in the back squeezed together to make room for the four new shadows. A mass of grey settled in the rear of the vehicle.

"*Kurati venelased*," Kalju growled, cursing the Russians. "They're taking them away."

A torrent of nausea curdled in Madli's stomach. "They're being arrested." She plunked down on the floor with her back against the wall. Perhaps the Kiiks were spies. As the notion formed, she didn't believe it.

A shot exploded outside. She dived onto her stomach. A scream pierced the quiet then was cut off.

"Don't look," Kalju whispered. "Keep your head down. If they spot you they'll come for you."

Limp and cold, she lay on the floor.

The truck motor rumbled to life and the vehicle roared down the street. The distance swallowed the noise until silence hung heavy in the summer night.

"They're gone," Kalju whispered as he peeked outside. "At least for now."

Madli lay motionless on the floor. Relief and tears came in waves. First, small waves that made her gasp, then larger waves that forced tears into a damp patch on the carpet. A final wave left her weak and thankful and happy. And guilty.

"We ... didn't ... help ... them." Each word was a separate breath. "We watched as they were taken away." Her body trembled as she gulped air.

"Maybe they were spies," Kalju said with no conviction.

Maybe. Perhaps. Probably not. Her flood of tears ebbed, but deep in the crevices of her mind she knew that even if the Kiiks were innocent, she wouldn't have helped them. Nobody could have.

Madli sat cross-legged on the floor. "What did they do wrong?" She feared the answer as she wiped her tears on her nightgown sleeve. "Were they bad people?"

"Probably only to the Soviet army," Kalju said. "Who knows why they were arrested. We may never understand." He turned his head. "And we'll never ask."

"How can soldiers take them from their homes in the middle of the night?" Her sleeves were already damp, so she grabbed the hem of her nightgown to wipe away more tears.

"Anyone can be arrested," Kalju said with bitterness. "They just need to be breathing."

"They were probably spies or government officials," Madli said hopefully. "It must have been serious for the whole family to be taken." She sniffled into her hem. "They wore heavy coats and boots. It's the middle of summer."

"They're being deported, probably to Siberia," Kalju replied. "What were you planning to do with that?" He gestured at tennis racquet. "Were you planning to volley back the bullets?"

Madli didn't laugh.

"There's nothing we can do." Kalju's voice sagged. "Let's try to get some rest." He headed back to the bedroom.

Madli followed him. When she saw Peeter fast asleep she thanked whatever sleep god it was that protected young boys.

Peaceful sleep for her was impossible. She tossed and tangled up the covers. Her bed was the same place she had left a short while ago. Now it felt lumpy and uncomfortable. Were they all sheep waiting for the Red Army to herd them to slaughter? There were tens of millions of young, strong Red Army soldiers armed with rifles, and maybe a million Estonians — and that number included grandmothers and infants. They had no chance. Resistance would earn a bullet through the head or worse.

Madli fell into a restless slumber and dreamt someone was knocking on the door. She opened it to see Stalin standing there. His eyes burned with the glorious promise of Communism and he looked exactly like his portrait in the school assembly hall. Thick slick black hair, caterpillar eyebrows, bushy moustache. *Come with me*, he said. *Your summer vacation will be spent in Siberia.* Madli wore only a nightgown and managed to grab a thin sweater and her suitcase before they headed outside. He led her to a truck that held a dozen quiet people. She shivered from the cold. *It's not your fault*, he said as he helped her into the back and placed her suitcase beside her. He waved to Madli as the vehicle sped across the icy tundra.

The dream of Stalin still churned in Madli's head as the first light of morning beamed through the window. Her ears strained to hear footsteps upstairs, small light footsteps that would tell her everything was normal.

There was only silence.

Kalju and Peeter were up so she slipped out of bed and dressed in yesterday's clothes. Her suitcase beside the bed reminded her to get her winter coat, heavy cardigan, and winter boots. With shaking hands, she fetched them from the closet and stuffed them in a large linen bag beside her suitcase. Just in case.

Madli wandered into the living room, peered out the open window and filled her lungs with sweet summer air. It was the kind of shimmering June day that made the long dark winter nights seem as far away as the moon. She strolled into the kitchen, where the boys were eating breakfast. Leftover potatoes and bread. In the last few hours, new shadows and wrinkles had developed on Kalju's face. His jaw looked moulded from limestone.

"Were they bad people?" She clapped a hand over her mouth. In her exhaustion she'd forgotten about Peeter's big ears, which listened to every word.

"Who?" Peeter's brow furrowed and he bit his fingernail.

Kalju's fork paused halfway to his mouth. "The Kiiks were arrested last night. Perhaps they were spies." He shrugged. "Eat your food."

Peeter stopped fidgeting. "Could we be arrested as well?" The furrow in his brow became a trench.

"Anything is possible." Kalju speared another potato.

"What if we became Communists?" Peeter asked. "Would we be safe? Uncle Stalin would protect us."

Madli and Kalju exchanged glances. Every cell in Madli's body quivered with fear. All the values Papa and Mama had embedded in her screamed against joining the Komsomol.

Kalju hit his fist on the table so hard the cutlery rattled.

"We're not lying, to the Soviets or ourselves. I forbid it and so would Papa."

Peeter stopped asking questions. He probably didn't want to hear more answers. His lower lip trembled and his blue eyes flooded with tears. Before Madli could move, Kalju pretended to flick a potato from the end of his fork at Peeter. "Who would want an annoying seven-year-old?"

"Except us, of course," Madli said with a smile for Peeter followed by a glare for Kalju. Peeter's childhood became shorter each day. When Madli was seven she played hide-and-seek with her friends and dressed her doll in the most beautiful clothes. His memories would be about arrests, deportations, and soldiers with rifles on the streets.

"Should we call Mama?" As the words left her mouth, she knew the answer. Even if Kalju said yes, she couldn't concern Mama.

"She'll worry," Kalju said. "I can take care of things." He squared his shoulders.

Madli nodded out of habit.

She remembered her mother's request to fetch medicine for Aunt Erika. The mere idea of going outside made her hands clammy. Her hands twisted her skirt. "I need to go to the pharmacy for Mama."

Kalju raised an eyebrow.

He didn't offer to go. That would be her idea of taking care of things.

People ran errands, went shopping, and met friends every day. "Stay with Peeter," Madli said. If she pretended life was normal, perhaps it would be. "I'll take the small streets." And hurry like the wind.

With a linen bag in her hand, Madli opened the apartment door, stepped onto the landing, and pulled the door shut. The noises from last night exploded in her head. Russian voices, thumping boots and the light footsteps of the Kiiks. A cold chill cascaded down her back.

Madli grabbed the doorknob.

Be brave, Papa's voice said.

What for? retorted Madli.

Slowly, Papa's voice pushed out the other sounds and her hand slipped off the door handle. It wasn't bravery that motivated her — more stubbornness and pride. She wouldn't slink back inside like a dog with its tail between its legs.

In the dim light, she examined the stairs going up. No trace of the night before.

Madli descended backwards and scrutinized each step down to the ground level. Nothing different. She opened the door to the street and stuck her head out. Looked left. Nobody. Looked right. No cars or trucks. Then left again as she stepped onto the sidewalk and pulled the door shut. The street surrendered no evidence of last night.

Madli walked over to the spot where the truck had parked, and scuffed her shoes on the road as if she could uncover evidence. Nothing. A couple of cars rolled by.

Her last chance to dash upstairs. A curtain fluttered in their second-storey window.

Facing one's fears was much overrated. Her pounding heart, sweaty palms, and wobbly legs made her feel like throwing up.

Madli placed one shaky foot in front of the other as she strolled down the cobblestone street toward the old town. The red tile of the medieval turrets peaked against the clear blue summer sky. A glorious day. Delicate summer scents tickled her nose, and the pastel-coloured buildings with their walls in shades of yellow, green, and pink made her smile briefly. The buildings stood unyielding despite countless invaders over hundreds of years.

She drew comfort from their solidness and sameness. Perhaps Estonia had a chance.

On any other day, Madli would have loved to go to the pharmacy in the middle of the town square. Countless footsteps had passed through its door since the early fifteenth century. As a young girl she pretended she was a sorceress shopping for supplies for her magic potions: maybe some mummy juice or burnt bees. Or better yet, burnt hedgehog powder, bat powder, or snakeskin potion. Today she fantasized about a brew to change the evil Soviets into wart-covered toads or slimy snails. A vision of toads jumping over discarded rifles tugged a smile to her lips.

Madli halted at the edge of the empty town square and peered around the corner. Three soldiers paced in front of the town hall. The scarlet hammer and sickle flag slashed the blue sky like an open wound. One solder lit a cigarette and flicked his match to the ground. Slobs. Mouth dry, she ducked behind the wall.

Walking across the wide open town square was out of the question. Being inconspicuous was the goal. She turned to double back onto the small streets that would deliver her close to the pharmacy door. Hugging the cold stone walls, she scurried along the winding streets. Almost at the last bend, the toe of her shoe caught in a gap between the cobblestone. She pitched forward, arms flailing. As she grabbed for the wall, from the corner of her eye she saw someone burst around the corner. Unable to regain her balance, she braced for the impact.

CHAPTER FOUR

The collision knocked the courage right out of her. Like a fly untangling itself from a spider's web, she thrashed to free herself from the stranger. Madli stepped back, heart hammering. It was a girl with dark curly hair.

"Madli, it's me." Sarah's kind brown eyes became serious. "What are you doing out alone? Didn't you hear what happened last night?"

The sight of Sarah calmed her heartbeat and breathing. Damp hands yanked her blouse into place while she repeated Sarah's questions in her mind. "No." The word stuck in Madli's dry mouth. Possibly the upstairs neighbours were famous spies and news of their arrest had spread. On the other hand, Sarah didn't know her address. "What happened?" She folded her arms across her chest.

Sarah's eyes darted around. "Come with me. I don't want

to talk in the middle of the street. Our shop is around the corner."

Sarah's voice carried such urgency that Madli nodded.

As they hurried along, Sarah continued in a low voice. "Last night the NKVD arrested hundreds of people and took them to the train stations. My father heard people were given merely minutes to pack. The soldiers told them they were being taken to Siberia."

Goosebumps prickled Madli's arms. More people arrested, not only their upstairs neighbours. She rushed to keep up with Sarah. She had to find out what happened even if it meant being late. An image of Kalju pacing the street in front of the apartment flew through her mind.

"Come, my father will tell you more." Sarah shoved open a heavy wooden door.

Madli waited by the front door of the candy store while Sarah hurried to the back.

"Papa," Sarah called. "Can you come here, please? There's someone I'd like you to meet."

As a child, Madli had thought the walls and floor were made of rich dark chocolate. Kalju let her believe it until her father told her the truth. The familiar sugary smell brought back memories of birthday parties, Christmases, and sticky fingers smeared with chocolate.

Sarah's father hurried out from the back of the store, wiping his hands on his apron. Dark curly hair sprinkled with grey and a worried expression in his kind eyes completed the resemblance to Sarah.

"Papa, this is Madli. I ran into her a few days ago," Sarah said. "I started to tell her what happened last night."

Mr. Goldberg nodded. "It is very bad. Hundreds, maybe thousands of people were dragged from their homes by the NKVD."

He tugged his fingers through his hair. "It's terrible. They were yanked from their beds."

A familiar nausea slithered into Madli's throat. "Where were they taken?" she managed to ask.

"The train station, either in Kopli or Pääsküla," Mr. Goldberg replied. "The platforms are filled with people being deported to Siberia."

"The trains haven't left yet." Sarah shuddered.

Pääsküla. Aunt Erika and Uncle Jüri lived near that station. Mama was there.

Madli's head whirled like a top. She was certain it would spin off into space. "How do you know this?" The details made no sense. Right now, not too far away, people were waiting to go to Siberia.

"My brother lives near Pääsküla station," Mr. Goldberg answered. "For days, he noticed empty cattle cars lining up along the tracks and wondered why."

"Early this morning, the knock on the door scared me half to death," Sarah interrupted. "My uncle came over to tell us that people are jammed together on the train platforms. They're still waiting to board. Men, women." Her gaze focused on the wall behind Madli. "Children, grandmothers and grand-fathers. Entire families standing with boxes and suitcases beside them."

Sarah's voice came from a distance, as though Madli were listening to a radio with poor reception. "Why?" she asked. The lump in her stomach became a boulder.

A flame ignited in Sarah's eyes. "These grandmothers, these ordinary people, these small children, are considered counter-revolutionaries."

"Traitors to the Motherland." Mr. Goldberg's lips compressed into a thin line of anger. "*Feh!*"

Madli didn't know what *feh* meant, but Mr. Goldberg's manner left no doubt.

"The so-called lucky ones have luggage with them. One lady wore only a nightgown." Sarah shook her head. "Imagine being put on a train to Siberia in a nightgown." Her eyes widened into brown orbs. "It's barbaric."

The smell of sugar and chocolate made Madli's stomach queasy. She couldn't muster any words.

Mr. Goldberg glanced at his watch. "My batch of candy is nearly cooked. If it burns, the Soviets wouldn't like it." His lips pursed as if to spit into the batch. "Be careful, Madli. Our world is not safe." He left through the back door.

Madli looked down at her feet, surprised they were still anchored on the floor as the world spun out of control. It was hard to believe they were in the same place as yesterday. How could so much happen in so short a time?

"It's so horrible," Sarah said. "We are all shocked." Her eyes became moist and pink as she held back tears. "Madli, be careful. Anyone could be a target."

"Nobody is safe." The words caused Madli's voice to crack and she swallowed hard. "You must be scared as well."

"We're leaving tomorrow," Sarah said. "I've been so sad, but I'm ready to go."

"Are you going ... on holiday?" Madli felt confused. It was summer, after all, and people had vacation plans.

"No." Sarah dropped her gaze to the floor. "We're leaving for a long time."

"Where are you going?" Madli asked.

"A small village outside of Leningrad. We're going to stay with relatives there." Sarah met Madli's eyes.

It was impossible not to think the worst in a world where children and grandparents were targeted for deportation and

Red Army soldiers burst into aparments in the middle of the night. Her imagination wove a dark story about Sarah, and these thoughts poured out of her mouth. "You're going ... to Russia? Are you a Communist? Or are you crazy?" The world spun faster. "Are you tricking me? Are you going to turn me in to the Soviets? Are you going to deport me?" Her voice, high-pitched and hysterical, rang in her ears.

"Of course not." Sarah placed her hand on Madli's arm. "Why would you think that?"

Madli snatched back her arm and folded them both across her chest. Doubt stormed through her mind. "You're Jewish." She waved a finger at Sarah's necklace. "You wear a gold star."

"We are Jewish. And Estonian. My father fought in the War of Independence in 1918."

The note of pride in Sarah's voice soothed Madli's nerves.

"Estonia has accepted our religion," Sarah continued. "Unlike the Nazis." Her eyes narrowed. "They want to exterminate all the Jews. *Judenfrei.*" She spat out the last word. "We're afraid of the Soviets, but more afraid of the Nazis; Russia is the lesser of two evils. The border to the west is closed so we'll go east." Sarah shrugged. "My mother's family live in the village."

"How can the Nazis be worse than the Soviets?" Madli asked. To go willingly to Russia was like walking into a blazing fire.

"Nazis hate Jews," Sarah replied simply. "The Soviets just hate religion."

The Soviets hate everyone was the response that leapt to Madli's mind. She couldn't decide if she was scared to be Estonian or glad to not be Jewish. Neither concept had crossed her mind before today.

Madli wrung her hands together. "I ... I don't know what to say. My brother is waiting for me and I'm so late. I must get home and tell my family."

From her skirt pocket, Madli dug out the Estonian *kroon* she'd found the other day. She pressed the coin into Sarah's palm, though she was positive she would never see her again. "For when you return."

The glimmer in Sarah's eyes and the warmth of her hand flamed a tiny ember of hope in Madli.

"Be careful," Sarah said in a hoarse voice.

"You too." Madli's voice cracked. A torrent of emotion choked her as she walked out the door.

Squinting in the bright sunlight, she stumbled, barely able to put one foot in front of the other. It was as though all her beliefs had been put into a bowl and, like eggs, mixed up and scrambled on a hot stove until they no longer resembled their original shape. Who was right and who was wrong? Who knew? Leaving Estonia had never occurred to her before; she'd always assumed the Soviets would depart and life would return to normal.

Her feet eventually took her back to the town square.

The pharmacy. The medicine.

Madli dashed around the perimeter of the square, up two steps and through the tiny door into the pharmacy. From her pocket she dug out the list and heard herself ask for the herbs, heard her mumbled words of greeting to her mother's boss, then her thanks. She grabbed the ingredients, stuffed them into her linen bag, and bolted back home via the small back streets, this time taking long strides and peeking over her shoulder.

Madli burst into the apartment, slammed the door shut, then locked it. "Kalju." She tossed the medicine on the hall table. "Where are you?"

No reply. Her imagination raced for answers. Arrested, bleeding, or dead in the bedroom. "Kalju!"

"In the living room," came the calm response.

Kalju sat at the small desk in the corner and Peeter was curled up on the sofa. "I saw Sarah and her father," Madli blurted out. "They told me what happened last night."

"What?" Kalju put down his pencil. "How did they know about the Kiiks?"

"No, no." Madli waved her hands. Her legs shook as the story gushed out, then slowed to a trickle. When she stopped talking, two pairs of wide eyes stared back.

Kalju's brows formed a single furious line. "You know what Stalin says." His lips went white. "'No people, no problem!'"

Madli winced. No people, no problem.

"Are we in danger?" Peeter asked with the largest eyes she'd ever seen on him. "Are we going to be deported? Because I don't want to leave even though I don't like this place." He glanced around the small apartment.

Madli motioned for Peeter to come over and hoisted him onto her lap. "There's no sense to any of this." The silkiness of his hair brushed her cheek.

Peeter, who usually wriggled out of anyone's grasp, wrapped his arms around her waist.

Another crescendo of panic came. Were they all in danger? What would happen to them? Were Mama, Aunt Erika, and Uncle Jüri standing in a train station in their nightclothes? What about Toomas and Grandpa and Nana? Her grip on Peeter tightened. A scream quivered deep in her throat.

Be brave.

She'd rather hide.

"We should call Mama. She must be frantic." Madli stated the obvious. "Maybe she's heard from Grandpa and Nana."

Kalju's eyes widened. Madli knew the same questions raced through his mind.

Peeter squirmed and she reluctantly loosened her grip. Scaring Peeter would accomplish nothing.

Kalju headed to the phone and picked up the receiver. "It's dead." He jabbed the buttons on the cradle. "Still dead." He replaced the phone in its cradle.

"Uncle Jüri is picking us up early tomorrow to drive us to the ferry in Rohuküla," Madli said. "We have to stay." The inability to call Mama gnawed at her. The phone lines were unreliable these days.

❖

Exhausted by the events and emotions brought about by the last two days, Madli spent the rest of the day packing and repacking her suitcase. The repetition calmed her nerves. She couldn't decide whether to tuck her winter coat in the bottom or put it on the top or perhaps hang it on the end of the bed for easy access. As she picked up her diary a picture fell out. Papa and her, standing beside a figure of that funny American character, Mickey Mouse, on the beach in Haapsalu when she was eleven. A hundred years ago. She brushed her fingers over Papa's face. A handsome man with light brown hair, a moustache that tickled, and hands that caught her when she fell. A better, safer time would come again. Madli had to believe that. Madli tucked the diary and two short letters from Toomas on top of Papa's manuscript in her suitcase.

After dinner, Madli lay on the living room floor, flipping cards in a half-hearted game of solitaire. They were going through the motions of a normal evening. Peeter was curled up at the end of the sofa with his one-eyed teddy bear. Kalju sat on the other end with an open book on his lap. As bedtime approached, the light outside deepened to lavender.

Her fears deepened as well. Would the Soviets make another pass? The picture of the Kiiks in their winter coats flashed through her mind. When she'd promised Mama she'd look after her brothers she hadn't anticipated the wrath of the Red Army. Madli had meant that she would cook dinner and make sure everyone packed for Hiiumaa. She'd been so scared today. What if she had to do something that really required bravery? She'd be a heap on the ground.

As the clock approached nine, Madli noticed she was wringing her hands like Mama. The hem of her skirt was twisted into a ball. Each insignificant sound caused her to wince. By the time the clock reached nine-fifteen she was pacing. To the window. Rain pitter-pattered on the sidewalk. Back and forth. Papa was in jail. Back and forth. The neighbours had been arrested. Back and forth.

Madli halted in the middle of the room. Were they on a secret Soviet list? Families of arrested people were targets themselves. The Soviets could arrest them simply because Papa was in jail. Never mind Papa's manuscript hidden in her suitcase. Possession alone was treasonous. Her father's name would make it doubly so. If it were found by the soldiers, none of them would make it as far as the door.

Her panic worked itself into a tornado of emotion. The manuscript was her secret, but it was no excuse to risk her brothers' lives.

"I don't want to go to bed tonight," Peeter whispered. He clutched his well-loved teddy bear. "I'm too scared."

Madli's mind raced for a solution. "I have an idea."

"Is it about becoming invisible?" Peeter asked. "Do you have a magic potion?"

"It's the next best thing to becoming invisible," she said. "We should sleep in the upstairs apartment tonight. It's empty, and the soldiers wouldn't come back to the same place twice."

"No." Peeter burrowed into the corner of the sofa. "That's strange. I don't want to go."

"It is strange," she agreed. "And possibly wrong on any other day." Despite the words, she was no longer convinced. All her life she'd been taught right from wrong and good from evil. None of those rules applied anymore. She craved black and white, not shades of ever-changing grey and cloudy morality.

"I'm not running from the soldiers." Kalju straightened up in the chair. "It's our apartment and I'm staying."

"We can be brave," Madli said, "or we can be smart."

"It's illegal," Kalju rebutted. "They'll arrest us for trespassing." His lips thinned into a line.

"How can it be wrong to save ourselves?" Madli asked. "Anyone with a fraction of a brain would say 'Yes, hide from those evil Soviets.'" Though she wouldn't admit it, she half agreed with Kalju. If they hid from the Soviets, they'd be giving in to their game. If they didn't, they could be arrested, deported, or executed. For the truth. Fine choices. "We could be right-minded people with high morals and get killed. Why take a chance? We leave tomorrow."

Kalju shook his head. "I say no." The stubborn slant of his chin reminded her of Papa. Both fought for their own truth, damn the consequences.

"I'm scared," Peeter said. His face crumpled as it did when a tantrum was brewing.

"And I say yes." The words fell out before she knew it. Arguing with Kalju was unfamiliar, but she had to protect them and Papa's manuscript. If Kalju found out, he'd make her burn it. She didn't want to share this precious secret with him. This was between her and Papa.

Kalju glowered at her, but his expression softened as he observed Peeter's face. "It's wrong."

Madli exhaled softly. "Peeter, it will be a big game of hide-and-seek." Soviet style. Her shoulders quivered.

"I don't want to be found," Peeter said.

"Exactly," Madli replied. "Go get your suitcase." She faced the full force of Kalju's glare. "Come with us," Madli said softly to him. "Think of Mama."

Kalju's silence told her he was.

"We're not safe. With Papa in jail, we're a target."

"I'm ready." Peeter appeared with his suitcase in one hand and his teddy bear in the other.

"We can't leave our suitcases here," Kalju said. "If they find them, they'll be suspicious."

Madli nodded. "I'll tidy up." She put away the dishes and organized the hallway. The apartment had to appear as though they'd left it days ago. Nobody home, no problem.

"Let's go, Madli," Kalju called from the front hallway.

"I'll be right there." In the bedroom, Madli picked up her suitcase and grabbed her winter coat, her boots, and Peeter's winter coat.

"Why are you carrying those?" Peeter asked as she stepped into the hallway.

"I hate to be cold," she replied. Especially in Siberia. The thought of her brother on a train in a shirt and short pants caused a shiver. "Here is yours as well."

"I don't need my winter coat in the summer," Peeter said. "It's too warm." He folded his arms and faced the door. "No!"

Behind his back, she rolled her eyes and stuffed his coat into the linen bag.

"Let's go."

Peeter scampered up the stairs first. Madli locked the door and followed him up the stairs, treading softly, taking care not to make noise. There wasn't a reason to be stealthy, but it felt better. One by one they arrived on the landing.

"How will we get in?" Peeter asked.

"The soldiers wouldn't lock up, would they?" Madli replied.

Kalju fumbled with the handle, one way then the other. The door clicked and opened. He stepped through the door.

The smell of stale cigarettes greeted her. "We mustn't stand in the corridor." Madli nudged Peeter over the threshold into the tiny hallway. The apartment layout was identical to theirs.

Madli peered around the corner into the kitchen. A red- and white-striped sweater lay draped over the back of a wooden chair. Four white bowls were set on the table for a breakfast that would never be eaten. She backed out and nearly knocked a picture off the wall. Her trembling hands straightened it out again. She clasped her hands together to stop the shaking.

In the living room, a standing lamp with a circular beige lampshade cast a wan glow over the striped velvet sofa, more brown than beige. Madli averted her eyes from the pictures and books on the shelves. There was no reason to understand more about the Kiiks.

"Why did you turn the lights on?" Madli moved to switch them off, then backed away. A family picture stood on the table beside the lamp. The Kiiks looked like nice people, people who lived a decent life. An ashtray held a couple of lipstick-stained cigarette butts.

"I didn't," Kalju said.

"Now what?" Peeter asked.

"Now we try to sleep," Madli said. "Or at least rest a bit."

"Or pretend to." Kalju paced back and forth.

Or they could sit up all night to listen for footsteps.

"Are they dead?" Peeter asked.

Probably not yet since they're still sitting in a train.

"I'll stay here in the living room," Kalju said. He sat down on the sofa and bounced his right leg up and down.

"I want to sleep under the bed," said Peeter. "So they can't find me."

"Good idea," Madli replied. Kalju would pace all night. "I'll join you on the floor."

Madli tiptoed into the bedroom with Peeter behind her. Her eyes stung as she took in the double bed with the yellow quilt torn back. White pillows edged with lace were rumpled with sleep. Three of the four dresser drawers were open with clothes spilling out onto the floor. A tiny white shirt lay on a wooden chair by the window. Clothes were heaped in the far corner. Pyjamas. She had an urge to straighten up the bed, to fold the clothes and tuck them away in the drawers. Instead she placed her winter boots beside the door.

Madli spread Peeter's winter coat on the floor under the bed.

Without hesitation, Peeter burrowed under the bed and curled up on the coat.

Madli positioned her coat beside Peeter's and collapsed on top of it. Two lumps bulged against the lower part of her back. She squirmed to remove the offending pieces from the pockets. The winter mittens Nana made for her.

"What are you doing?" Peeter whispered.

"I found these." She showed him the blue and grey mittens decorated with geometric patterns and narrow stripes at the wrist. "Are yours in your pockets also?"

Peeter fished around in his coat pockets and pulled out his pair, similar to Madli's except for being red.

"Peeter," Madli said. "These are magic mittens."

"Mittens are not magic," Peeter retorted.

Madli pulled them on. "Nana wove enchantment into them." She hummed a spinning song. "Nana sang this special song to fill the yarn with powerful magic."

Peeter put on his mittens and examined his hands. "Hmmmm."

He rolled onto his side and fell asleep clutching his hands together.

Madli removed her mittens, rolled onto her stomach, and retrieved her diary and pencil.

> Saturday, June 14, 1941
>
> Kallis Papa,
>
> Tonight we play hide-and-seek. Soviet style. We hide, they seek. We're hiding in the Kiiks' apartment so that the Soviet soldiers won't find us. They arrested hundreds of ordinary people last night and took them to train stations.
>
> Nothing in my education or experience has taught me to lie, steal, or manipulate. I'll learn if we're to survive. The rules of life have changed and I don't understand them.
>
> You and Mama taught us how to make good decisions, be good people, and do good things. How will this help me now? We've done nothing wrong and everything right. And now? None of it matters.

Madli laid her head down, exhausted. She couldn't lift her head to write the next sentences.

> I pray for morning.
> I pray Mama and Aunt Erika and Uncle Jüri are safe.
> I want to go to Hiiumaa.

Madli closed the diary, tucked it in her bag, and slipped on the mittens. A little magic couldn't hurt. She hummed the spinning song. Her eyelids closed despite her vow to keep them open.

CHAPTER FIVE

Sunday morning, Madli squinted into bright sunlight. A strange ceiling above. A hard floor below. She was still in the Kiiks' apartment. Her ears strained to hear anything unusual. Typical morning street noises filtered through the window.

The vague smell of damp wool seeped into her nose. She pulled the mittens off her sweaty palms and tucked them back into the coat pockets.

"Peeter, wake up! It's morning. The magic mittens worked." Madli sprung to her feet. "Come on! We're leaving."

"I'm going to wear these every night." Peeter stretched.

"Great idea. Come on. Let's go." Last night she couldn't wait to leave their apartment and this morning she couldn't wait to go back. The last image of the Kiiks, bundled up and huddled in the back of the truck, haunted her. If she kept changing locations, the Soviets wouldn't find her.

Madli tugged on Peeter's coat so hard she almost flipped him onto the floor.

"Hey," he protested.

The Kiiks' apartment was left as they had found it. Bowls on the table, clothes scattered on the floor, and an empty cup in the sink.

The door latch clicked and Madli mouthed silent thanks as she followed the boys down the stairs.

Back at the apartment, Peeter ran to his room.

Kalju's sunken eyes told her he hadn't slept much. "Did you hear anything last night?" he whispered.

Fear clutched her throat. "No," she said. "Did you?"

Kalju shrugged. "Don't think so." He dropped his suitcase by the door. "Let's eat."

Not sure whether to believe him, Madli headed to the kitchen. She boiled water for porridge. The boys appeared in the kitchen as the scent of barley rose from the pot. They wolfed down their breakfast in silence.

Worry nibbled at her. Any minute heavy boots would pound up the stairs. "We need to leave soon. Let's wait for Uncle Jüri outside."

At ten o'clock, they waited on the empty sidewalk with their suitcases. Where was he? Minutes ticked by. The worst outcomes invaded Madli's mind. Aunt Erika and Uncle Jüri had been deported. Mama as well.

"Perhaps there's a problem with traffic," Kalju said. "Or with the truck. He's had to repair the engine a number of times." His foot tapped on the sidewalk.

Madli realized that her hands were doing the same thing Mama's did when she was nervous. Squeezing and kneading her fingers, wringing and grasping and clasping. She forced her hands into her pockets. A black car slowed down, while the woman passenger stared at them. Madli's hands popped out of her pocket. The next vehicle could be a truck filled with Soviet soldiers. A small lump rolled in the bottom of her stomach. Just before the lump in her stomach turned into a boulder, a vehicle roared around the corner with the unmistakable figure of Uncle Jüri at the wheel. The truck ground to a halt and he unfolded himself from the driver's seat. Uncle Jüri was built like an outhouse: tall, solid, and often smelly, which he didn't seem to notice despite his large, craggy nose.

Ignoring his breath-stopping smell, Madli flung her arms around him and felt her stomach settle to its new normal: a queasiness that threatened to intensify at any threat. "I thought you wouldn't come. How's Mama?" she asked. "And Aunt Erika?"

Uncle Jüri quickly untangled himself to fetch the suitcases. "Your mama's been frantic," he said over his shoulder as he threw their luggage into the back. "Our phone didn't work. Jump in. I've got to get back and do a delivery."

"Have you heard from Nana and Grandpa?" Madli boosted Peeter into the back of the truck.

"Yup." Uncle Jüri climbed into the driver's seat.

The one small word turned her knees soft. There was no point in asking more questions; Uncle Jüri wasn't a big talker. Madli scrambled in and settled alongside the lumber with Peeter. Kalju squeezed into the front beside Uncle Jüri.

As the truck rumbled towards the outskirts of the Tallinn, all appeared normal. There was no blood on the roads or people screaming for help. A well-dressed man in a dark suit walked calmly into a grocery store. A young mother pushed a stroller. Two elderly ladies with hats chatted on the sidewalk.

A lone seagull hovered above them, then swept over the red tiled roofs and old walls of Tallinn to vanish out to the sea. Madli wanted to be that bird and swoop over the train stations to see with her own eyes. Before she soared out to sea, she'd crap on every Soviet's head.

Uncle Jüri turned onto his street. The truck had barely stopped when Madli jumped onto the sidewalk. She was halfway up the path when the door of the house flew open and Mama burst out.

"Thank goodness you're safe." Mama stroked Madli's hair, kissed Peeter, and then crushed Kalju in a hug. Her hands flitted from one child to another. A brief touch, a brush on the arm to make certain they were real. "Let's go inside." Mama shepherded them into the first-floor apartment.

Inside, Madli's eyes adjusted to the dim light in the hallway. Her nose twitched with the smell. A dank, sour smell of buttermilk and cat pee.

Aunt Erika had settled her immense frame on the living room couch. Not for the first time, Madli wondered how she and Mama could be sisters. Big, small. Brunette, blond. Uncle Jüri, Papa. Three cats, three children. Madli crowded into the living room with everyone. She sat on the floor, cramped at her mother's feet.

"Why would the Soviets do this?" Madli rested her head on her mother's knee. "They've taken old people and children and families. Why are these people being punished?"

"Hundreds, maybe thousands," Mama said, her face pale. She twisted the hem of her dress.

"How could they be a threat to society or a danger to anyone?" Madli asked. "Who could they hurt?"

"The Soviets want to eliminate the culture, not only arrest government officials and other bureaucrats." Mama's eyes were deep wells of sorrow. "They want to remove any trace of Estonia. Who is the future of a country? Its children. If there are no children, there is no future." A sigh escaped. "Who holds the memory of the culture? The mothers and grandmothers. If they are gone, so are the memories."

Icicles dripped down Madli's spine.

"The trains haven't left yet," Uncle Jüri said. "I drove by the station this morning."

"Oh, my dear Lord." Mama's hands flew to her face. "What are they doing?"

"Waiting."

For hell. For hope. For a miracle.

"People tried to slip them food or water, but the guards wouldn't allow it," Aunt Erika said.

Mama stroked Madli's hair, something she hadn't done since Madli was a little girl. For a moment, Madli closed her eyes. The knot in her stomach eased as the conversation about deportations and arrest faded into the background.

"Kalju, can you take this bread and herring to Mrs. Raud?" Aunt Erika asked. "She lives off Pärnu Maantee at twenty-five Lauliku Tänav. Poor woman lives alone and I haven't been able to take her meals since I fell. Selma, can you get the food, please?"

Reluctantly, Madli moved away from Mama's warmth. Her mother came back with a package of food wrapped in a towel and handed it to Kalju.

Madli stood up, eager to escape the claustrophobic room. "I'll go too. Mrs. Raud will want to chat. Come on, Kalju."

"Be careful," Mama said. "Go straight there and come right back. It won't take long."

Kalju and Madli walked down the road past silent wooden houses with lace drapes drawn. At the corner Kalju stopped. A defiant gleam shone in his eye. Madli followed his gaze down the road — the other way, the way toward the train station.

"No, Kalju." Madli's hands flew up in protest.

"Come on. We won't go to the actual train station. Remember the laneway over there? We can see the station through the bushes." Kalju took another step.

Madli grabbed his shirttail. "No. It can't possibly be safe." She leaned back to brace herself.

"They can't pull people off the streets as they walk by." Kalju shook her hand away, while balancing the parcel of food.

"Right." Madli yanked on his shirt. "Instead, they'll come into your house and drag you out."

Kalju ignored the comment. "I'm going with or without you. And you can't go back alone. It'll take a minute. I need to see. Just see." He gazed at her hand. "Let go."

Madli nodded, while her stomach churned. She couldn't let him go alone. If anything happened she could run for help or scream. She let go of Kalju's shirt, her heart pounding. The sensible part of her didn't want to see the people. The other part, the part of her that didn't believe even the Soviets could be so cruel, that part needed to see the people waiting at the train station.

At the end of the lane, Kalju parted the lilac bushes.

Madli inhaled the fresh perfume of her favourite flowers, then placed a hand on Kalju's shoulder to steady herself as she peered through the gap.

A cattle car. Big and brown. Two vertical sliding doors stood partway open. The top half of the door showed a gaping hole into the dark interior. No people. Perhaps they sat on the floor of the wagon.

Her eyes darted left, then right. Dozens of wooden cattle cars snaked along the track as far as she could see.

Her fingers dug into Kalju's shoulder. "How many cars are there?" His shoulder shrugged.

What could the Soviets want with all these Estonians? Did the soldiers not have families of their own? Mothers, fathers, sisters or brothers?

Madli focused on the car in front of her. The people inside had been there for over a day.

Faint strains of a song floated down the tracks. The words drifted along the tracks, over the cattle cars and out into the ether where no one would hear them. *Ma tahaksin kodus olla.* It was the saddest sound Madli ever heard.

"I hate them," Kalju said in a whisper.

His shoulder was like granite.

Hate. As a child she hated carrots and spiders and ugly shoes, and that was the extent of her hate. Today she glimpsed the vastness of emotion that hate could be. This kind of atrocity deserved hate, begged for hate.

Madli squeezed in beside Kalju to get a better look.

A small blond head appeared. Wide eyes met hers over the bottom half of the door. A girl with long golden braids stared straight into Madli's heart.

Madli gripped Kalju's arm. The little girl's gaze packed the same wallop as the punch in the stomach she'd received on the playground in first grade. It delivered a blow that left her breathless.

"What?" Kalju swatted at her hand. "Stop it."

"She's watching us." Madli's voice cracked. She pointed a shaky finger.

"Do you have food?" the girl asked quietly.

Madli shook her head. Kalju stiffened beside her.

"We've been here for a couple of days. I'm hungry and thirsty," the girl said in a composed voice.

No words formed in Madli's mind. The impossibility of the situation paralyzed her. The girl was the same age as Peeter. Too young to starve on a train to Siberia.

"We have the food for Mrs. Raud," Kalju whispered.

Madli met his eyes, eyes filled with a sadness she'd never seen before. He was waiting for her to decide. Logic evaporated; she nodded. It was the right thing to do, a good thing. A really dangerous thing.

The distance was a few yards. "How do we get it to her?" Madli scanned the tracks. No guards to be seen but that meant nothing.

Kalju surveyed the distance. "Can we throw it to her?"

"What if we miss?" Madli asked. "It goes to waste. Or we get shot by a Soviet guard." She couldn't walk away with food in her hands and the memory of that plaintive voice.

"We have food," Madli whispered to the girl in the cattle car.

"Food." The voice held hope and wonder. "Really? You have food?"

"How can we get it to you?"

"Be careful," the girl said. "There are guards around. On the ground, in the trees."

Madli reconsidered. The consequences were unthinkable. She let the bushes close over her face.

"Wait. Don't go away. Please," the girl begged. "My mother will have an idea."

In the silence, Madli heard the sound of water flowing onto the ground. She peered through the branches. A thin stream of liquid trickled from underneath one of the cattle cars. Someone was peeing onto the track. A shudder gripped her. All those people and no washrooms.

The girl returned. "We have string. If I throw it to you, can you tie the food to it?"

What if a guard caught them? Madli wanted to run, back to the house, across the sea, to the moon.

"We should try," Kalju whispered.

They had to try. Madli nodded.

"Yes," Kalju and Madli whispered simultaneously.

The string sailed through the air. Madli willed it to land within range. It dropped to the ground a few feet away.

A tiny "Oh" came from the train.

"*Kurat*," Madli cursed.

There was nothing between them and the girl but the sharp gaze of hidden Soviet soldiers.

No one moved.

Madli exchanged glances with Kalju. To stride out into the open to retrieve the rope was out of the question and it was too far to reach with a stick. The pale yellow string taunted her. A thin cord between her and a cattle car.

"Oh," the girl said. A pair of arms enveloped the girl.

The muffled crying tore at Madli's heart. "Let's go," Madli said. A Russian soldier could pounce on them. Fright shoved in beside her desire to help. "It won't work." Hot tears welled and the rope blurred.

Kalju backed out of the bushes. Leaves snagged Madli's hair as she followed him.

"God bless you and keep you safe," came a soft grown-up voice. "Remember us and write about our tragedy. Our people's tragedy."

Madli couldn't look back. An unimaginable sadness invaded her soul as she walked along the sidewalk. Each step pounded the horror into her further.

Kalju's shoulders hunched as he focused on his feet. He rubbed his eyes and she wondered if he was wiping away tears.

They delivered the food to a grateful Mrs. Raud then scurried back to the apartment. While they walked back, Madli couldn't shake the feeling of Red Army eyes following her. She peeked over her shoulder a dozen times. No one in the streets. No one in the trees. Aunt Erika's house came into view. Madli sprinted toward the door. She pulled it open and inhaled the odours of cat pee, old food, and old people. A palace. A castle. A home.

"We were getting worried," Aunt Erika boomed.

Mama gave them a curious glance as they walked into the living room. "Mrs. Raud must have talked your ear off."

Madli nodded and glanced at Kalju, his face pale. No mention of the girl passed their lips. She curled up at Mama's feet and rested her head on her knees. Despite the loud conversation and presence of her family, Madli felt totally alone in a world where she had no control, simply luck.

Later that night, while Kalju and Peeter slept and the cat snuggled at her feet, she wrote in her diary.

Sunday June 15, 1941

Kallis Papa,

We're safe for now. The trains overflow with innocent people, and just as easily it could be us. We're helpless. No one will come to our aid. No one listens to us. We can't even help each other.

I hate the Soviets. How can they be so cruel? And why? They have power and millions of people. Why bother with us?

You're fascinated by the politics of history, the catalysts for war, the battles fought, the land lost and the power gained. Today I realized that individual tragedies are just as significant as the losses on a battlefield. People can't be forgotten because they were deported or arrested. People like the little girl. People like you.

"Remember us and write about our tragedy," the mother said.

I will. I must.

Writing the words on the page provided Madli a sense of power, control, and clarity. The power of the written word had brought down nations, started wars, ended wars, shaped history. Perhaps one day it would make a difference.

CHAPTER SIX

All night the little girl's voice haunted her. Madli told herself she couldn't have made a difference. No one could.

After breakfast, she stood beside the truck with Kalju and waited for Uncle Jüri. The sweetness of lilacs in bloom brought back memories of summers on the white sand beach in Haapsalu, a new light blue swimsuit and sugary drinks. As Madli inhaled the delicate perfume, in the distance the train started to move. The fragrance of the lilacs combined with the memory of the stench of Soviet soldiers. No more swimsuits for that little girl on the train.

Chug ... chug ... chug.

The steady pulse of the train wheels spinning fell into rhythm with her heartbeat. The summer warmth seemed distant as she imagined herself hugging her knees on a wooden floor inside one of the dark cattle cars with no food or water. Or hope. A shiver travelled down her spine and her legs trembled.

Madli searched for Kalju's eyes, but he ducked around the other side of the truck.

Chug ... chug ... chug.

How long would the people be on the train? How many would survive?

"Come eat some porridge before you go," Mama called from the door.

"I will," Madli said automatically. She knew she couldn't put a bite into her mouth.

Chug ... chug ... chug.

When would the little girl eat? When would any of them eat?

An eternity later the noise faded into the distance. The train was gone.

East toward Siberia.

A tiny ray of happiness pierced Madli's heart. The train was gone and none of her family were on it.

Hope shattered. What if Papa was on a train?

An hour later, truck packed, porridge not eaten, Madli stood entwined in Mama's arms. Her fierce hug squeezed the air out of Madli's lungs and tears out of her eyes.

"Be safe," Mama said. "You and the boys are all I have."

Rough hands cradled Madli's cheeks.

"A blue eye from me and a brown one from Papa, so you know how much both of us love you."

"I can stay with you in Tallinn," Madli said. As much as she loved Mama, she didn't mean it. She couldn't wait to leave Tallinn. Was Toomas still in Hiiumaa? As a seventeen-year-old boy and a fiercely outspoken supporter of independence, he'd be a prime target for deportation. Was there no end to worry?

Mama's hands patted Madli's cheeks as if she were considering the suggestion. "No, I'll be fine. I need to stay with Erika.

Nana and Grandpa need you on the farm. Besides, I always think it's safer on the island." She took a breath and Madli knew what she was going to say. "Nowhere is the sky so high and the earth so large, nowhere are the woods so endless. Nowhere are the birches so white, so green the moss, and the flaming sunburns in the evening so red." She'd heard Mama's favourite part of von Vegesack's poem numerous times.

".What if Papa comes back?" Madli whispered.

"I'll send word immediately." A sad smile flickered over Mama's lips. "You go now. Uncle Jüri is waiting." She tugged Madli's sweater back into place.

Madli hesitated. Mama's nails were bitten to the quick. Before the Soviets arrived Mama had beautiful long nails, painted red when Papa and she went out to dinner or the theatre.

"Go." Mama nudged Madli. "Grandpa and Nana are waiting for you."

Madli climbed up into the back of the truck with Peeter. Kalju sat in the cab with his window down. "Bye, Mama," Madli called. She waved in big arcs. Tears in her eyes doubled everything. Days ago she had wanted nothing more than to spend her summer in Hiiumaa. Now she feared she'd never see Mama again.

The motor sputtered then turned over. Uncle Jüri clunked the truck into gear and spun the car toward the main road.

West toward the sea.

PART TWO

CHAPTER SEVEN

Hiiumaa Island, Estonia

The ferry to Hiiumaa ploughed through the grey sea. Madli leaned over the railing, mesmerized by the churning water alongside the boat. The water swept past the stern and mingled into the waves, as though the boat had never passed through it. Like the trains at the station. Gone, leaving an empty platform behind.

A summer-cool Baltic breeze whipped her hair across her face and dried the splash of fresh tears. If only the gust could carry away the memories of the last days. Instead, the wind forced the images into every crevice of her mind. Thousands of Estonians deported to Siberia. Families, mothers, children, herded into cattle cars, rolling east across the tundra, while she breathed fresh air. How long would her luck last? Was the knot in her stomach permanent?

The island drew close, all thick forest and craggy rocks. A

handful of people had gathered on the pier. Madli's lips parted in the tiniest of smiles.

Red and white mittens grasped the railing beside her. "There are Nana and Grandpa," Peeter announced. He waved.

Kalju appeared on her other side. "Hard to miss Grandpa. He's always the tallest one."

"I see Nana's blue kerchief." Madli dragged her hair back with one hand and with the other shielded her eyes from the sun. The knot in her stomach eased at the sight of her grandparents. She tugged off her sweater and brandished it in long sweeps. Grandpa and Nana waved back. A wide grin eased onto her face.

Who else was on the dock? One boy with blond hair stood tall, causing her stomach to flutter. Could it be Toomas? As the boat approached the dock, the boy morphed into a stranger. The stomach flips subsided. Blond-haired boys were as common as mushrooms. As if a farm boy would take time from his chores to drive hours to meet her.

Another thought gnawed at her: perhaps he wasn't on the island. The notion scalded her heart.

The ferry nudged the dock. As the crew secured the lines, Madli scampered with Kalju and Peeter to the exit ramp. On the pier, Grandpa stood tall as a birch tree while Nana swayed in the strong breeze. The gate opened and Madli ran off the boat onto solid ground toward her grandparents. She'd never understood people who kissed the ground upon arriving somewhere, but now, had she been alone, she would have been on her knees, lips to the land. Madli flung herself into the arms of her grandmother and kissed her soft wrinkled cheek. Nana's arms enveloped her like thick cords of rope.

"Is everyone safe?" Nana whispered.

Madli's chin bobbed against Nana's shoulder. "Mama and Aunt Erika and Uncle Jüri." Madli's imagination exploded with horrible scenarios. Toomas forced into the back of a truck. Toomas jammed into a cattle car. Her heart thumped as she opened her mouth to ask about him.

"Thank goodness," Nana said. "It's terrible, so terrible." Madli felt herself pushed to arm's length as Nana examined her. "Let me look at you." Steady blue eyes surrounded by crinkled skin inspected Madli. "You're pretty as a rose." Satisfied, Nana turned to Kalju. "Some fattening up for you, young man." Nana pinched his cheek. "Good farm food will take care of it."

"Did you bring your muscles, Kalju?" Grandpa clapped Kalju on the back. "I need all the help I can get. The hay is almost ready to bale."

"Yes, sir. Can't wait," Kalju said, almost enthusiastic.

Madli gaped. To get him to lift a dish at home was an accomplishment.

Grandpa grabbed Madli's suitcase. "I won't be able to get a word in all summer." His face creased into grumpy folds, but his eyes twinkled.

"Peeter, you've grown like a weed." Nana squished Peeter into her embrace, then began inspecting him. "My goodness. Those pale cheeks. A little sun and you'll be brown as a berry. What are you doing with winter mittens? There's no snow in July, silly boy."

"They're your magic mittens, Nana," Peeter replied. "They saved us from the Soviets, so I'm going to wear them all the time. Can you make me socks and a sweater as well? We're going to need a suit of magic."

A crease wrinkled between Nana's brows. "Magic saved you from the Russians?" Her eyebrow lifted. "Thank God." Her gaze swept the gathering of people and landed on the soldiers at the end of the dock. "We'll thank God if the Soviets can't hear us." She faced Peeter. "Tell me about that magic later." The crease deepened. "We were so worried. The phones didn't work, and then the next day they rang and rang. I was beside myself with worry."

Nana barely stopped to breathe when she was in a mood. Madli wouldn't be able to get a word in until next month. Her feet scuffed the gravel.

"Good grief, woman!" Grandpa growled in mock frustration. "We'll be here 'til next Sunday if you don't stop hassling the youngsters. There are cows and chickens waiting. We live on a farm, remember?" He winked at Madli. "Finally, we're getting help from these city children. Thank goodness I won't be the only one up at dawn. Now I'm hungry; you brought food along, didn't you Mother?"

Grandpa's mouth curved at the corners like Papa's. Madli's breath caught in her throat. Since his arrest, she'd stored memories of Papa deep in the back of her mind, but Grandpa's crooked grin dragged them out. How would she not burst into tears each time she saw Papa's smile on Grandpa's face? She turned toward the breeze.

Grandpa lumbered toward the wagon with the boys at his side. Nana grasped Madli's hand and whispered, "Our world has gone completely mad." A firm hand stroked Madli's hair.

Madli took a breath to ask her about deportations on the island, but Nana flitted over to Kalju. Madli chewed the side of her finger. Biting calmed her nerves.

At the wagon Peeter flexed his arm and a small muscle flickered under his shirt. "Grandpa, when do I get to drive the wagon? You promised. I'm much taller and stronger this year."

Grandpa's lips twitched as he towered above Peeter. "You'll have no problems controlling those horses, but today we need to make fast time. Jump up and let's get home." Grandpa tossed the luggage into the back of the wagon, helped Nana onto the bench, and heaved himself into the seat beside her.

Madli climbed into the back along with Peeter and Kalju. No chance to ask Nana anything for a couple of hours until they got to the farm. Grandpa clicked his tongue and the horses trotted off.

In the rear of the wagon, Madli lay on her back with the sweater tucked under her head. What was Mama doing right now? Where was Toomas? In an open field or jammed into a cattle car? Even the warmth of the sun couldn't soothe her swirling thoughts. With every hoof clop, her thoughts bounced between Mama and Toomas. She forced herself to focus on the beauty of Hiiumaa. A ribbon of blue sky ran between towering pines and spruces. A multitude of scents tickled her nose. Pine, sea, summer wildflowers, daisies, bogs, fresh grass, the dung of sea birds. Hiiumaa smelled green, not grey like Tallinn.

Gravel crunched and she lifted her head. Only the Soviet army drove cars on the island. A Jeep with two Soviet soldiers shot by in a spray of pebbles.

"Are there lots of soldiers here?" Peeter watched the Jeep disappear.

"Not as many as Tallinn," Madli lied. Hiiumaa had thousands of Red Army soldiers stationed on the bases guarding the island. As long as they kept to their bases and didn't steal blond boys from farmhouses.

Madli tapped her foot against the side of the wagon. She wanted to forget. She wanted an ordinary summer. It wasn't admirable or brave, but all she wanted was two months of normal farm life with fresh food and her friends. Nothing could be done against Soviet aggression. Uncle Stalin dispersed candy, deported people, and arrested at will. No people, no problem, no options.

Madli laid her head back on her sweater and dozed as Nana rambled on to Grandpa.

She was jerked awake by Peeter's voice when they arrived at the farm. "There's Pontu!" The wagon shook as he hurled himself toward the dog.

Madli peered over the wagon railing. The large black and white dog streaked across the farmyard, barking madly at the intruders. Peeter froze, while the dog circled and sniffed. Within seconds, Peeter passed the sniff test and Pontu licked his hands.

The original thatched roof farmhouse from the late nineteenth century appeared ancient next to Nana's dream home, a two-storey wood house Grandpa had built a few years earlier. The new house had a front veranda, a walk-in pantry, custom-built kitchen cupboards, table and chairs from the Luther furniture factory, a grand piano, and a green velvet sofa and loveseat — among other modern decor items Nana had persuaded Grandpa to buy. On the vast property the old barn, sauna, and storage buildings dotted large fields of tomatoes, potatoes, beans, wheat, and flax. The forest encircled their little kingdom, while the ribbon of road pierced it and led them out of the forest to the village. A small path twisted down through the trees toward the Baltic Sea.

The tiny village boasted forty-two chimneys, twenty of them saunas.

Madli jumped out of the wagon and held out her hand for Pontu to sniff. The black and white dog tentatively approached her, then slobbered over her hand. "You remember me, don't you?" She scratched his floppy ears.

"Put your things away," Nana said. "I'll make tea." She headed inside.

Kalju and Peeter went to the upstairs bedroom. Madli hurried to store her suitcase in the summer bedroom, a separate room at one end of the house with an entrance off the porch. The door didn't creak this year, but otherwise the room was the same. Never mind that the area was so small she could practically touch the walls with outstretched arms; it was pure luxury after months of sharing a room with the boys. A straight-back wooden chair. A snow white pillow resting on a green blanket bright with embroidery. Hooks on the back of the door for her clothes. A small chest of drawers. She tugged open the window to eliminate the musty winter smell. Unpacking and blissful solitude could wait until later. She had to find out about Toomas. Maybe Nana wanted to protect her from bad news.

By the time Madli had crossed the porch, she'd convinced herself that Nana was hiding a terrible secret. The kettle whistled as she burst into the kitchen, set to interrogate Nana.

"Just in time," Nana said. "Sit down, *kalli*."

Madli twisted the arms of her sweater around her waist and plopped herself into a kitchen chair beside the window. Same worn kitchen table and straight-back chairs. Outside, Peeter threw a stick for Pontu. Nana placed a mug of tea on the table. The smell of it made Madli's stomach flip. Words filled her mouth, but she didn't dare utter them.

Kalju walked into the room and headed directly for the bread box. "Where's Valter?" He tore off a chunk and stuffed it into his mouth. "Mmmmm."

"He went to Kärdla, but will be back in time for the Midsummer party." Nana tied an apron around her waist. "He won't tell you, but I know he can't wait for your summer visits." Nana beamed at Madli longer than necessary. "I'm going to fetch potatoes for dinner."

With Nana in the pantry, Kalju sidled up to Madli, still chewing. "Valter looks forward to your visits."

"Our visits." She ignored his tone. Kalju's new interest in matchmaking was annoying.

"He's such a nice boy and such a hard worker," Kalju said in a high-pitched voice.

She cuffed him on the arm. "And practically my cousin." Grandpa and Nana had raised Valter after his parents were killed in a farm accident. As they would for a son, they ensured that he received a good education, a warm home, and lots of love.

"He's not related." Kalju walked toward the stairs.

Nana dumped the potatoes on the kitchen table, while Madli found an extra knife to help. Her stomach churned as she fumbled for a way to ask the question.

"Nana." Madli's voice broke. "Was anyone ... taken ..." She swallowed. "Deported from here ... near here ... from the village ... anyone I know?"

Nana's knife stopped. "Oh, Madli." Her eyes glistened. "Yes, lots of people."

Madli didn't feel the cut until she noticed drops of blood on the potato.

"Madli, you poor girl." Nana scurried for a rag and wound it tight around Madli's finger. "Come. Sit down."

Madli crumpled into the wooden chair. "Who?" Her heart galloped.

"Valter told us about the deportations the next morning when he came back from the village," Nana began. "A truck collected the people and took them to the same pier we were at."

"Who?" Madli leaned forward toward Nana. She felt as though she stood in the centre of a hurricane. Any moment, the wind would howl. "Who was taken?"

"Oh, my." Nana shook her head. "The Lepiks and their three children, the Niits, and the Öiges." An expression between resignation and hatred flashed across Nana's face. "We were lucky."

"The Rebanes?" Red leaked through the thin rag. Funny, there wasn't pain. "What about the Rebanes?"

"They were lucky, also." Nana said.

Madli didn't hear anything after that. As her blood warmed, she welcomed the sting of the cut. Nana kept talking about other families. Madli didn't care. Toomas was alive and minutes away. A grin snuck onto her face until she noticed Nana staring at her. She rearranged her face into a serious expression. "It's tragic, Nana." It was the strangest sensation. Of course, she wasn't happy that people were headed to Siberia, but she was ecstatic that Toomas was not. She'd see him tomorrow.

Monday, June 16, 1941

Kallis Papa,

I'm so happy nothing has changed at the farm. Nana talks nonstop, while Grandpa pretends to be cranky. Peeter has become fast friends with Pontu. It's good to see him with a dog, playing and carefree.

I breathe easier on the island, surrounded by forest and the sea, rather than the ever-watchful eyes of Soviet soldiers. The only eyes observing us are those of the birds, the sheep, and the cattle.

Your manuscript is tucked safely under my mattress. I pray for an ordinary summer.

CHAPTER EIGHT

Sweaty fingers in scratchy wool. Madli, half asleep, yanked the mittens off and slid them under her pillow. She burrowed under the covers, snug in her tiny room, and savoured the fresh tang of the Baltic Sea air mingled with the crisp scent of spruce and juniper. Out of habit, her ears searched for strange noises. Cows mooed, birds twittered, a rooster crowed.

Madli peeled off her nightgown and tossed it on top of her winter coat, draped over the footboard of the bed. She dressed quickly. Anticipation lightened her step as she crossed the porch toward the kitchen. "Hey, Pontu," she whispered to the dog basking in the morning sun. "I'm going to see Toomas today after breakfast." Her stomach rumbled as the scent of porridge beckoned her inside.

"Good morning, Nana." Madli sat down at the kitchen table. "Weren't those cupboards brown last year?"

"I finally persuaded Grandpa to paint them a lighter colour," Nana said. "I wanted to make the kitchen more modern. *Talu Perenaine* has so many great ideas for decorating. I've kept all the back issues. Grandpa thinks grey is the only colour, but this is 1941. Modern decorating calls for light colours on the walls and tasteful wallpaper." She stirred the porridge. "Though now, all of that seems frivolous."

Madli nodded. "Where is everyone?"

Nana pulled a bowl off the shelf. "Your brothers are helping Grandpa milk the cows and feed the pigs." She scooped a steaming mound of barley porridge, plunked it into the bowl, and handed it to Madli. "The milk is on the table."

Madli added milk and picked up her spoon, anticipating the first bite.

Clack, clack, clack.

The sound was sharp, the rhythm steady. Army boots. Soldiers marching.

Madli went numb. The spoon slipped from her fingers and plopped into the porridge bowl.

Clack. Clack. Clack.

Her legs tensed, ready to bolt. Madli perched on the edge of her chair. "Nana, what's that noise?"

"What noise?" Nana wiped a dish with a tea towel.

Clack. Clack. Clack.

In time with her heart. Thump. Thump. Thump.

"That. Noise."

Nana tilted her head. Smiled. "Storks, dear. They're clacking their beaks."

Madli's whole body relaxed. Lucky storks, not unlucky army boots. Her fingers touched her forehead. Damp.

"You're not used to farm noises yet," Nana said. "Grandpa needs a stork nest on the farm for luck."

Madli's heart stopped pounding. With steady fingers she picked up the spoon. Thoughts of soldiers vanished. Not at the farm. Madli scooped the porridge into her mouth and didn't stop until the bowl was empty. As she washed her bowl, Grandpa stomped into the kitchen and headed to the cupboard.

"Can't find anything." He opened the cupboard.

"Dishes are not meant to be on display." Nana continued her mending.

"Cups are meant to be found so I can drink." Grandpa found a mug and filled it with tea. "Madli, come to the woods with me. These creaky old knees are swollen and noisy today. Ma, where's the sack?" He gulped down the tea.

Not one of Grandpa's expeditions. Not today. A list of excuses rolled through her mind.

"In the barn," Nana answered. "As usual."

"We need to find the biggest anthill and freshest birch leaves. You'll hold the bag, while I shovel the ants."

Madli managed a nod. The only thing she wanted was to see Toomas. Grandpa assumed she was still a little girl, interested in concocting medicine from ants, vodka, and earthworms.

"Ma, pack some food, please." Grandpa lifted an empty linen bag off the hook.

"Madli, can you get a jar of strawberry jam for me?" Nana asked.

"Yes, Nana." An afternoon wasted searching for ants. Madli shuffled to the pantry. It was filled with Grandpa's remedies. Red earthworms covered with vodka had been baked in the sun to form a powerful salve for Grandpa's rheumatoid knees. Madli searched for strawberry jam. "Eww!" Right behind the snake vodka. In the spring he'd catch a viper, stuff it in a bottle and pour vodka over it.

Papa used to find the biggest, fattest earthworms for Grandpa. The image of Papa as a little boy pulled tears from deep within her. She shook off the vision and returned to the kitchen.

"How long are we going to be gone?" Madli handed the jar to Nana.

"Not too long," Grandpa replied.

Nana stuffed four loaves of bread, potatoes, cheese, and a hunk of dried fish into the linen bag. Grandpa added a bottle of milk.

How hungry could Grandpa get in a couple of hours?

"Start the water boiling for when we get back," Grandpa commanded.

Nana responded with a mock salute.

"I'm going to need it for the ants." He crooked a finger at Madli. "Let's go." With the sack full of food tossed over his shoulder, Grandpa was a summer St. Nicholas.

"Come, Pontu."

The wild strawberries by the side of the path were still green. In a few days they'd morph into small red bombs of flavour. Madli licked her lips in anticipation.

The trail into the the forest disappeared as the trees grew closer together. Moist dark soil, early summer flowers, spruce, pine, and juniper mingled into a forest bouquet of summer scent. Tall trees soaked up sounds and a dense quiet pervaded except for the madding hum of mosquitoes. The bugs gorged on her bare skin. After waving wildly, she broke off a large leafy branch to swat them. She developed a steady rhythm with the branch. Over the left shoulder, a swing back over the right shoulder, a couple of quick brushes along her legs.

Madli's imagination turned to Toomas. Would he be taller and leaner after the long winter? Would the summer sun have kissed his blond hair? Would his lips twist in that adorable lopsided grin? Would the sound of his deep voice turn her knees to *sült*?

Sunlight coaxed a million shades of green from the trees, and mushrooms the size of porridge bowls peppered the forest floor.

As their feet trampled the duff, Madli heard conversation. Her ears strained, but the only sound was Grandpa's footsteps scuffling on the forest floor. She stopped. Immediately, mosquitoes landed on every bit of bare skin. Flailing madly, she scrambled away from the vicious insects.

Moments later, words drifted through the trees. Men talking, then a high-pitched laugh, definitely not male. Her fingers flew to her mouth and she chewed on the side that had almost healed over.

Madli sprinted up to Grandpa. "Shhh, listen. There are people talking." Her voice came out coarse from a dry mouth. "Let's go." A tug on Grandpa's sleeve produced no reaction. "What are you waiting for?" She was set to bolt when she glimpsed Grandpa's face. His lips drew up at the corners.

"We came to help these people," Grandpa said calmly.

"In the middle of the forest?"

No reply. Sticks crunched and twigs snapped as he lumbered through the forest.

Madli's nose picked up the unmistakable scent of roasting meat. A faint path of crushed pine needles and leaves led towards a small clearing where the sun beamed down on men and women and an open fire. Three children, Peeter's age or older, kicked a ball. Two blond girls darted between the pine trees like fairies in the forest. They laughed, then took off as another boy jumped out from behind a spruce. Six children and five adults. Underwear and trousers swayed on a line strung between two trees. A handful of lean-tos dotted the area. Two were built into the side of a small hill. The others were barely noticeable between the trees.

Pontu barked, clearly as confused as she was to see people in the middle of the forest.

"Who are they?" Madli asked.

A lean man with tousled blond hair strolled over, white shirt crumpled, hands outstretched.

Pontu growled.

"Our special delivery is here." The man clasped Grandpa's hand. "Arvo, you're a good man." A smile broke across his weathered face.

"Yes, yes. You'd do the same for me." Grandpa opened the sack and pulled out a loaf of bread.

"Of course." The man beckoned for others to join him. "Though not everyone would risk their life."

Another man, thin and unshaven, strode over to them. No smile from him.

Two women joined them. One was as old as Nana and the other was Mama's age. "You're so kind. How can we ever repay you?" the younger one said. "My children will have milk and bread. Thank you." Her smile, though tired, made her pretty.

Grandpa reached into his linen bag, pulled out the food, and handed it to the women. They embraced the bounty the way one might a baby.

A vision of the eyes in the cattle car flashed through Madli's mind. These people were evading the Soviets.

"Come, we shot a boar the other day. Have a taste." The lean man gestured toward the fire.

Grandpa held up his hand. "No, thank you. We're searching for smaller creatures today." He gestured to Madli. "Madli, my granddaughter, is here for the summer."

She gave them a smile.

The unshaven man didn't relax his gaze. "Can she be trusted?"

Madli nodded, throat tight. It wasn't clear what she was being trusted with.

The man flicked his hand. "Really? If I were a Russian soldier with a gun, you'd tell me everything."

Absolutely. She'd blurt out what she ate for breakfast.

"She can be trusted." Grandpa's tone left no room for doubt.

Madli met the unshaven man's glance again, this time with more confidence. His expression softened enough to indicate he valued her grandfather's words.

"What else do you need? Food, clothes?" Grandpa swung the empty sack over his shoulder.

"We'll pay you, as soon as we can." The lean man hesitated. "A bit of beer would go down well."

"Thirsty, are you?" A grin spread over Grandpa's face. "Next time."

"We're not going anywhere," the man said. "Not with the Soviets poking around. We're comfortable." He gestured to the group. "It's much quieter here in the forest." He clapped Grandpa on the back and shook his hand. "God bless."

Madli caught up with Grandpa as he strode back into the coolness of the forest. "Why do they hide in the forest? And what can I be trusted with?"

"Both Jaan and Mihkel were officers in the Estonian army," Grandpa explained. "Prime targets for deportation. They won't take chances with the Soviets, especially after what happened last week, so they've moved their families into the forest."

"He's afraid I'd tell about their hiding place." Madli glanced around expecting someone to peek out from behind a tree.

"The forest can keep its secrets and so can you," Grandpa said. "For us, woods are a sanctuary. The Soviets will get lost and fall into a bog before they find them."

"Are there more people hiding in the forest?"

"Almost certainly."

Dead leaves rustled as she kicked a small rock. Would they be forced off their land to camp in the woods like animals, while the Soviets drank the milk from Grandpa's cows and ate the jam in their larder? Anger bubbled, but a wave of sadness washed it away. She wanted to forget about the Soviets. Resignation dropped over her like a wet cloak. Foolishly, she'd imagined that summer would trump an occupation. Despair slithered back.

"Aren't you afraid?" she asked. "Why aren't you hiding in the forest?"

Grandpa halted. His blue eyes sparked. "Afraid? Yes, I'm afraid of many things. Afraid of the Soviets crushing the Estonians. Afraid of never being able to sing our national anthem again. Afraid I'll go to my grave with the Soviet flag flying. We can't outrun the Soviets on an island so we need to outsmart them." His gaze shifted to a spot over Madli's left shoulder. "Look! Over there!"

She turned.

An ant nest, at least a foot high, created a massive dome on the forest floor. Ants wriggled along the forest floor, creating the appearance of a large brown scarf. Madli stepped back. Ants with brains the size of a pinprick could sting viciously.

Grandpa circled the anthill. "Thousands. Like Soviets invading Estonia." He chuckled at his own joke. He handed the sack to her. "Hold this."

Madli held the bag with extended arms. According to legend, plants harvested at Midsummer contained miraculous healing powers; perhaps the ants held stronger magic as well.

Grandpa attacked the mound with his shovel. A waterfall of ants poured out. Quickly, Grandpa tossed shovelfuls of dirt and ants into the bag. A few big clumps and Madli twisted the bag shut. Grandpa flung a rope around the neck of the sack and pulled it tight.

They hurried back to the farmhouse with their capture. Over the outdoor firepit, water bubbled in the cast iron cauldron. Grandpa dropped the sack into the pot. Madli winced at the innocent ants being boiled to death. A silly notion. The world would be unchanged minus a few ants.

"There we go," Grandpa said with satisfaction. "It'll soak the rest of the day. Before my bath, I'll add fresh birch leaves." He grinned. "I need to jump high over the Midsummer bonfire Sunday night."

"Do you need me anymore, Grandpa?" Madli stepped toward the road to Toomas's farm.

"Thanks for your help, Madli." Grandpa poked the mixture.

Nana appeared on the porch. "Oh, Madli, you missed Toomas."

"What?" Madli's feet fused to the ground.

"He dropped by on his way to Kärdla." Nana smiled. "He wanted to say hello. He'll be back in time for Midsummer."

"Oh," came out small and soft. Jaanipäev was an eternity away.

Tuesday, June 17, 1941

Kallis Papa,

The game of hide-and-seek continues on the island. Families hide deep in the forest from the Soviet machine, afraid for their lives. People are determined to outfox the Red Army. Are they cowards for hiding or smart for saving their families?

How long can they stay in the forest? They rely on the kindness of people like Grandpa and Nana to bring food and supplies. But what if someone betrays them? One of the men looked at me as though I'd take this information to the nearest Soviet. Of course I wouldn't, but someone else might.

We should all hide in the forest so there is no one left to arrest. Perhaps the Soviets would give up and go away.

CHAPTER NINE

By the end of the week, Madli's skin glowed golden, her feet hadn't touched a pair of shoes in days, and her appetite rivalled Kalju's.

Tomorrow was Jaanipäev, the celebration of Midsummer. Madli's favourite party.

And she would see Toomas. Finally.

On Jaanipäev, the longest day of the year, the sun rimmed the earth so that darkness never occurred. At sundown old fishing boats were ignited and set adrift. On the beach, massive bonfires blazed late into the night. When only cinders of the bonfire remained, boys would soar over the pile of hot ashes and collapse laughing into the sand. Last year, Toomas, with long legs, flew over the coals. Valter, heavier and clumsier than the other boys, scorched his feet as he jumped over the embers.

In the afternoon, Madli tucked birch twigs mixed with blue

cornflowers into a vase and set it in the middle of the long kitchen table. Birch brought luck and they needed no end of luck. She wiped her brow. Grimy from working and itching with mosquito bites, she couldn't wait for the sauna later in the day.

Around five o'clock Grandpa said, "Nana's at the sauna. I lit the fire hours ago so the rocks should be heated through."

Madli gathered her clean clothes and a flax towel, and headed over to the old building. Made from logs, the structure had two rooms, a small dressing room and the hot sauna. In the dimly lit dressing room she took off her clothes, folded them, and laid them on the bench.

Madli tugged open the door to the hot room, a small, dim cave lined with cedar. A fire, fed from the other side of the wall, heated the large stove covered with rocks. Two rows of wooden benches lined the wall. Shadows danced in the hazy heat. As her eyes adjusted to the dim light she saw Nana on the upper bench, her naked body already glistening with perspiration. Madli perched on the edge of the bottom bench. She felt like a dragon inhaling its own fiery breath.

"I could use a bit more heat," Nana said.

Words of protest caught in Madli's throat as Nana took the copper ladle, filled it with water from the wooden bucket beside her, and cast it onto the hot stones. The water sizzled and vapourized as it hit the rocks. Immediately a wave of heat rose, twisted around the ceiling, and draped itself over them. Madli bent over to gasp cooler air close to the floor.

"Ahhh, much better." Nana breathed deeply. "Come up here. You'll get frostbite down there." She chuckled.

The surge of heat scorched Madli's throat and nostrils. "I'm fine. Really." She held her breath to avoid burning her lungs. A few seconds later she gasped for air. She tried shallow rapid breaths which left her panting like a dog. Sweat cascaded from her pores and dripped to the floor. The first sauna of the summer took getting used to.

"Time for the *vihta*," Nana said a few minutes later. "I'll go first."

Beating each other with birch leaves was a sauna custom Madli usually loved, but she'd forgotten Nana's penchant for heat. A large whisk made from dried birch leaves soaked in a wooden bucket beside her. The water softened the birch leaves, making them smooth and pliable.

Nana stretched out face down on the top step, while Madli stood up on the bottom bench and grabbed the *vihta*. She wished for a wet washcloth to hold over her nose and mouth to cool the air. Shallow breaths, Madli told herself as she beat Nana's legs and back with the *vihta*.

Thwash, thwash, thwash.

Birch scent mingled with cedar as pink suffused Nana's glowing skin. Seven thwashes from shoulders to toes. Seven thwashes from toes to shoulders. Nana's backside was a drum and Madli beat the *vihta* in a lazy tempo.

Finally, Nana said, "Your turn."

Madli replaced the *vihta* in the wooden bucket to moisten the leaves. Nana came down and Madli climbed up to the highest step. Madli gingerly lowered herself onto her stomach on the warm wooden bench. She rested her head on her forearms and closed her eyes. The wet leaves rustled as Nana picked up the *vihta*.

Thwash, thwash, thwash.

The wet leaves thumped up and down her back and legs, tingling as the rhythm hypnotized her into relaxation.

Afterward, they cooled down in the dressing room. Nana sat on one bench. Madli sat on the other with a towel wrapped around her body. Following a sauna she felt like a snake that had shed its winter covering. Her new skin was polished and silky.

"Grandpa says there are no illnesses in the world the sauna can't cure." Nana's skin glowed.

"Except Communism." Madli mentioned the people hiding in the forest. "Have others taken to the forest?"

"The Vahtra brothers and their families are from a nearby village. Both the men are strong partisans." Nana reclined against the wall. "It's dangerous times for them. Hard to say how many others have taken refuge in the forest. People don't talk much. Anyone could be a Communist."

"One of the men was concerned I'd tell the Soviets their location," Madli said.

"Can't be too careful," Nana said. "One day the soldiers come for you because a neighbour complains about your pig on their property."

"What if Grandpa was a Communist?" Madli attempted to untangle her hair.

Nana laughed. "He wouldn't dare!" She rubbed her skin dry. "Though there are a few we wonder about."

"Why would anyone want to be a Communist?" Madli worked the comb through her hair. Tomorrow her hair would gleam when she saw Toomas.

"Well, fear is a good reason," Nana said.

"Fear of what?"

"Fear of being on the losing side. If they join the Communists, they won't be killed by the Red Army," Nana explained. "Hand me the cream. Of course, they'll die in other ways." She placed a hand over her heart. "In here." She rubbed cream on her face. "Power is another reason. Men who couldn't get a job shovelling out a barn are suddenly officers in the Soviet army. They'll shoot themselves in the foot before they'll shoot anyone." Nana ran her comb through her long grey hair. "Or they actually believe all the Communist propaganda. It's tempting to believe we're all equal and the world could be a better place if everyone was a comrade." She pulled out tangles with her fingers. "Of course, Stalin doesn't want to be my equal any more than I want to be his."

"Or they believe in candy." Madli mentioned the recruitment tactics in Peeter's class. "It's tempting for Peeter. He wonders if we'd be safer."

"They're impressionable at that age," Nana said. "When other children have things you don't, you feel left out. The Soviets are clever. Children want to belong. No one wants to be different or stand out at that age. The fact that we don't have candy makes their offer of sweets more tempting."

"Survival," Madli added.

"Survival isn't a bad motive. Lots of smart idealistic people have gotten themselves killed for a belief. Can't do much good if you're dead." Nana massaged cream into her feet.

"So, lying to survive is okay." Madli pulled on her underwear. Papa believed the Estonians had survived for thousands of years because they were so stubborn. They'd nod to their current ruler, then do everything in their power to overturn them.

Nana snorted. "If lying is the worst thing you do to survive, things are not so bad." She found her underwear. "We all fight, only with different weapons."

What kinds of weapons could she fight with? Madli's knowledge of history and literature couldn't be classified as dangerous. Fluency in Russian, German, and Estonian wouldn't stop any soldiers. Her skill with sewing, piano, and volleyball wouldn't scare anyone. She could hardly rally bullets back and forth with a tennis racquet.

"Your father fought with words," Nana continued. "His words

outlined the true history of Estonia, not the one presented to the world through Soviet eyes. The Soviets said we voluntarily joined the USSR. Hah." Nana sputtered. "They staged our elections last year, put in a puppet government, and pulled our strings tight. And so we dance." Her mouth pulled into a line. "His expertise and knowledge is lost. Over the last few years his lectures and articles were read and respected by scholars in Paris, Stockholm, and London. And because of that ..."

"Papa would never lie, so they had to arrest him." Madli squirmed as she remembered his manuscript. "What if he had finished his book?"

"The Soviets would have burned it." Nana finished dressing. "Come. Time to go prepare supper and let the men use the sauna."

Madli laid plates for dinner on the table when the door slammed and unfamiliar footsteps strode into the kitchen.

"Sorry, I was held up." The handsome young man kissed Nana's cheek. "I'm not too late for sauna? The men are still there, aren't they?" A smile lit up his dark eyes and softened his chiselled features. "Hello, Madli. Good you're here for the summer."

Madli gawked. Last year's plump seventeen-year-old boy had been sculpted into this year's eighteen-year-old man. The dim light found the angles of his cheekbones and deepened his chocolate eyes. A wrinkled white shirt barely contained his broad shoulders.

"Valter." Madli gaped. She recovered her speech. "Yes, we're here for the summer."

"I'll talk to you after sauna," Valter said. "Supper is almost ready so I need to rush." He headed upstairs.

Her eyes trailed him as he walked away. When had Valter

become so good looking? She'd never considered him attractive. Last year, he'd barely been able to heave himself over the bonfire.

Nana observed her with an amused expression. Warmth crept into Madli's cheeks.

"He's become a fine young man." Nana sliced rye bread. "My worry was for naught. Poor child. To have his parents killed so young. That kind of grief lasts a lifetime and I was concerned he'd grow up feeling lost and out of place." She placed the slices in a basket. "He's been like a son to us. So responsible and helpful."

Quiet, awkward Valter had morphed into smiling, attractive Valter. Madli laid the cutlery precisely, rearranged the flowers, plumped up the pillows on the sofa, and fussed over the dishes. She fluffed her hair in the hall mirror, thankful her skin glowed golden after days in the sun.

An hour later, the men and Peeter stomped into the kitchen. The sauna had stoked their appetites. As they wolfed down the meal, Madli snuck a peek at Valter across the table of half-empty beer glasses. She'd spent each summer of her life with Valter and always considered him a cousin. Being tongue-tied with him was a new experience, though the alternative was to say something silly. The salted herring lingered on her tongue, so she took a swig of Grandpa's freshly brewed birch beer to wash away its taste.

Grandpa devoured the last of his bread. "Is there more?" he asked, searching the table. A crumb fell to the floor. He bent down, picked it up, and kissed it as peasants had done for hundreds of years. "Bread is sacred and we can't waste a crumb."

"Can't waste the beer either." Kalju tossed the last drops down his throat.

"Madli," Valter said, "how is your piano playing?" He pushed his chair back. "There hasn't been anyone to sing with during the winter."

"I haven't played much lately." Soviet marching tunes and patriotic songs didn't appeal to her.

"I'm sure you haven't forgotten." He headed toward the piano in the living room. "Kalju, can you handle the mandolin?"

Madli squeezed beside Valter on the piano bench. After months of not playing, wrong notes echoed. His shoulder rubbed against hers and the clean scent of his freshly washed hair tickled her nose. Her concentration wavered. His rich baritone caressed her right ear as he flipped pages for her, leaning close to swing each page across.

Madli sang. Songs from her childhood. Estonian folk tunes that beckoned tears to her eyes and fear to her heart. Songs they'd be arrested, deported, or killed for if the Soviets heard them. It felt daring and brave to hurl the words into the tranquil night air.

As they finished the last song, Valter edged closer as he turned the page, close enough to exhale the final note on her neck. Light-headed, she held the final chord.

"I'll meet you at the shed tomorrow," Valter whispered. "We'll take the bikes to the village picnic. The others can go in the wagon."

Madli nodded, keeping her eyes on the music though she had finished playing.

"Good. See you at nine." He slid away.

Madli kicked herself for agreeing. It wasn't her plan to arrive at the picnic with Valter. Not with Toomas waiting.

Saturday, June 21, 1941

Kallis Papa,

In preparation for Jaanipäev I've washed every window in the house, swept out every corner, and dusted Nana's countless knick-knacks.

Kalju has taken an uncharacteristic interest in dragging logs and sticks to the beach for our bonfire tomorrow night. One of the few times he's exerted himself in physical labour. You'd be amazed at his strength.

Peeter's contribution to the festivities is chasing chickens, rabbits, and goats. It's so good to see him play.

The joy of ordinary summer activities.

I can't wait until tomorrow. Midsummer will be the best celebration ever.

CHAPTER TEN

The next morning, Madli scrutinized her reflection in the mirror. Her bronzed skin brought out the flecks of gold in her brown iris. A light blue linen shirt complemented her blue eye. Long blond hair was swept off her face by a hairband. Her skirt hovered about her knees and she tugged the waistband lower.

A flock of butterflies fluttered in her stomach.

The dew on the morning grass tickled her toes through the slats of her leather sandals. Wet leather squeaked in the quiet as she strolled toward the shed, smoothing her skirt with damp palms.

Two bicycles leaned on the fence. The early sun highlighted sparks of hazel in Valter's eyes and made his long dark lashes gleam. Rolled-up white sleeves emphasized muscular tanned forearms.

Madli's butterflies flapped wildly.

"Let's go." Valter swung a leg over the bike. "Race you to the graveyard."

"What?" A detour would make them late for the picnic, but he was already down the road, the bike spitting gravel. Madli tucked her skirt around her and pedalled down the road, faster and faster until the wind swept her mouth into a wide grin. Gravel crunched and bits of rock hit her shins like hungry mosquitoes as her legs pumped vigorously to catch up. Last year she had beaten him in their bicycle races.

A few minutes later they reached the graveyard. Headstones and iron crosses lay amid large shady trees. Valter coasted over to the fence and dropped his bike beside a cluster of flowers. He scooped up a handful of daisies and cornflowers.

Madli dropped her bike beside his. Her hands flew to smooth her hair. "We're going to be late." Impatience crept into her voice. To arrive at the picnic with her hair windblown and her blouse sweaty annoyed her.

"Ten years." Valter's eyes grieved for his parents who were buried in the corner under two tall oak trees.

Madli sighed as they strolled over to their grave. While it was customary to visit the graves of loved ones on Jaanipäev, timing would have been better after the picnic.

Valter laid the flowers in front of his parents' grave. He traced the date with his finger. "I don't come here enough."

"Such a tragic accident," Madli said. The memory of the actual accident was hazy. Something about horses bolting, the wagon overturning and trapping them underneath. She'd been five years old and had never seen a dead body, much less two at the same time, so when the bodies were laid out in the sauna it was unforgettable. Valter's father had been on the top bench and his mother had lain on the bottom bench, both shrouded with a sheet since the accident had disfigured them.

"For years I hated Midsummer because it reminded me of their death." Valter pushed a lock of unruly brown hair from his eyes.

"Oh." Since the arrest of her father, Madli understood the experience of utter loss. To be suspended in a state of disbelief no one else could comprehend. Sympathy welled for the young boy who'd lost his parents.

"Valve and Vladimir Novikov," Madli said softly. "She used to bake delicious jam cookies." The vision of a laughing auburn-haired woman tempting her with a cookie flashed through her mind.

"Not all Russians are bad." Valter's voice challenged her to disagree. "My father was a good man. Or at least my mother thought so. An Estonian marrying a Russian couldn't happen now."

Madli didn't respond. People didn't want to be associated with even a trace of anything Russian. "Don't tell anyone, but I enjoyed Russian history, despite the fact it was forced upon us." She gazed at the gravestone. "Russia had czars and gold and power. Estonia had serfs and peasants and manor houses. I wish Estonia had a king or queen, or at the very least a princess." She held her hands over her head to mimic a crown.

"Estonia does have lots of frogs," Valter said with a grin.

"Frogs?"

"Remember the fairy tale of the princess who kisses the frog?" His mouth curved. "The frog becomes a prince. We have lots of frogs."

"Amphibians are hardly the same as royalty," Madli said. "Do you talk to her?"

"Who?"

"Your mother." She ran her hand over the gravestone. "Do you ask her advice? Is her voice still in your head?"

"I'm not one to talk to dead people, but I try to honour their memory." Valter avoided her eyes.

"With my father..." A lump gelled in Madli's throat. "I've always wondered why people say 'rest in peace.' For me, not knowing whether Papa is dead — or alive, or in prison, or in Siberia — is worse. I can't talk to him if I don't know where he is. If he was in a grave, I could bring him flowers and I could tell him how things were going. Ask his advice and pretend to listen to him."

"Have you heard anything?"

"Last we heard he was in jail. For being an enemy of the people. But with the recent deportations, who knows?" Madli shrugged and her vision blurred with tears. She headed toward the bikes. "Race you to the picnic."

Madli pedalled furiously, eyes wide, counting on the wind to dry her eyes.

The village green was packed with familiar faces. Madli nodded and waved as she coasted over to the fence. Her eyes locked on the massive swing swaying back and forth. The swing platform was at least twice the size of Nana's dining room table, and a dozen young people were standing on it. In previous years, her friends would meet at the swing to talk, drink, and sing for hours.

Where was Toomas? She rested her bike against a tree.

"Kalju and Peeter aren't here yet. I'm heading over to the swing." She flung the words in Valter's direction.

It had been ten months since she'd seen Toomas. During the bitter winter nights, her dreams had been kept alive with the memories of last summer. Her feet dragged as uncertainty trickled into her mind. Why would he still be interested in her?

Acting like a naïve fifteen-year-old wouldn't help. Confidence was the key. Toomas liked her city sophistication, her love of books, and her sense of humour, though she couldn't think of anything funny these days.

Madli plastered on a smile and strode toward the swing, scanning the crowd for the right head of blond hair, for the familiar shoulders.

Toomas stood at the near corner of the swing platform sandwiched by two girls, one with two long braids. Madli's heart sank with a thud. The girl spun around. It was his sister, Silvi, with longer hair. Madli's heart flipped back. Silvi caught her eye and poked Toomas. Madli waved back like a five-year-old at a parade. She approached the swing, conscious of her worn shoes and too-short skirt. Hardly the clothes of a stylish city girl. Her hand dropped.

"Hi, everyone." The drone of conversation and the creaking of the wooden swing drowned out her words. Shouting, she asked, "Is there room for me?"

"Hey, city girl." Toomas grinned as he wooshed by, hair messed. His tanned skin made his blue eyes crystal. "Are we swinging too fast for you?" Even with the to and fro of the swing, his eyes held hers.

Her smile radiated. "Of course not."

"We can fit one more person," Toomas said. "Jump on." His hand reached for hers. Hands that ploughed fields and milked cows and built barns. Effortlessly, she floated onto the platform. Her chin grazed his broad shoulder. Just the right height. Leaner and more muscular than last year, the glint in his eye caused her knees to dissolve. She devoured the contours of his face. Full lips curved in a slightly crooked smile. Straight blond hair tousled by the wind. The barely noticeable scar on the side of his chin and the slightly-too-large ears. Words were impossible; she could only grin like a fool.

Madli was shoved full into his muscular chest as the swing

dipped and creaked. A hot blush rose from her neck as she peeked over her shoulder. Into Valter's dark, irritated eyes.

"Room for one more?" Valter said with an edge to his voice.

Madli's length pressed against Toomas. Her skin glowed as if she were in a sauna.

"Two more," Kalju said right behind him. "I could have crawled here faster. The horses knew Peeter had the reins."

Now that Madli was facing Toomas, the small hollow of his tanned throat mesmerized her. She focused on the top button of his shirt, hoping her cheeks didn't flame crimson.

"Let's see how high we can go with all these people on the swing," a boy said.

A chorus of "*Ja*" came, mostly from the boys.

Her one hand groped for the corner post. The other clutched Toomas's solid arm. With over a dozen people jerking and rock-ing, the swing picked up speed. The wood rasped and groaned as the platform glided back and forth. Her legs tensed. Toomas's arm secured her waist as they went faster and faster. Higher and higher. Each oscillation whisked away her winter worries.

"Whee!" Madli screamed in joy against his chest. Warm summer air and complete happiness filled her.

The swing creaked and groaned to a halt. Reluctantly, Madli relaxed her hold on the wood and unclasped her hand from Toomas's arm. She tossed the hair out of her eyes. "What fun!" The spark in Toomas's eyes teased another grin out of her. "I've waited all winter to do that."

Toomas widened his eyes as he tightened his arm around her waist. "So have I."

Heat blasted across her face.

"Did you hear that?" Valter asked from over her left shoulder.

"No, what?" Madli only heard the blood rushing in her head.

"Don't pump the swing," Valter said.

"Why?" Toomas asked.

Madli half-turned toward Valter. "We just started." She clipped the words.

"Attention! Attention, everyone!" a man bellowed through the murmur of the crowd.

"Shhh!" Valter said. "Listen."

"Someone probably wants to make a speech." Madli flicked her hand dismissively. "How wonderful it is to be together, what a lovely day it is, and so on." She rolled her eyes.

"I think ... yes ... that's Mr. Part," Valter said.

"It would be impossible to have a gathering where he didn't make a speech," Madli remarked.

Mr. Part, dressed in his starched Sunday best and every inch the village elder, waved one arm high in the air. "I need your attention for a very important announcement." Mr. Part's voice boomed through a megaphone. "*Silencium.*"

The crowd settled.

Toomas casually rested his hand on Madli's shoulder. The heat of it seared through her shirt. The longer the speech, the better.

"We've had extraordinary news." Mr. Part cleared his throat. "Germany has invaded the Soviet Union."

A gasp rippled through the crowd. *Germany has invaded the Soviet Union*. The words were clear, but Madli was too stunned to grasp their meaning.

Mr. Part held up his hand as he waited for the crowd to fall silent.

"*Issand Jumal!*" Toomas exclaimed. "Unbelievable!" His fingers dug into her skin.

"In a pre-dawn offensive, Nazi troops pushed into the USSR from the south and west, with a third force making its way from the north towards Leningrad."

The Nazi army was marching toward Estonia. Madli imagined

the sound of thousands of black army boots hammering the ground. Forward! March, two, three, four. And the sweet sounds of the Soviets scuttling back to Russia. No more sickle and hammer. Welcome back to the blue, black, and white.

"At oh-five-hundred Greenwich Mean Time, an hour after the invasion began, the Nazi Minister for Propaganda, Joseph Goebbels, went on national radio to read a proclamation by Adolf Hitler promising that the mobilization of the Nazi army would be the 'greatest the world has ever seen.'"

Would the Nazis drive the Soviets out of Estonia? Papa would be released from jail. The possibility of freedom made her lightheaded.

Toomas gripped her other shoulder.

"But we've always disliked the Germans," Valter said in a tone between hope and annoyance.

"Don't we dislike the Soviets as well?" Kalju's lips pursed.

Madli held a finger to her lips. "Shhh!"

Mr. Part continued. "The Soviet radio announcement asks for all vacationers to return to their place of work. Go home. Listen to the radio to find out more details."

Her euphoria evaporated. No! Not back to Tallinn. She wouldn't go. Summer had barely begun. Tears of fear and frustration burned her eyes.

Mr. Part stopped, took a breath, and held up his hand to silence the crowd. "The party is over."

CHAPTER ELEVEN

"Is this good or bad?" Madli murmured.

The Nazis wouldn't want Estonia. After driving the Soviets out of the Baltics they'd walk away. Perhaps the nightmare was over. Madli clapped a hand over her mouth, afraid her ideas would fly out and find their way to the wrong person. She faced Toomas. The crystal blue of his eyes had frozen to ice.

He jumped off the swing and held out his hand to help her down. "I'll walk with you over to the wagon. Silvi, tell Mama I'll be there in a minute."

Valter touched her waist.

"I'll meet you at the bike." Madli threw the words over her shoulder. Without waiting for a reply, she took Toomas's hand and hopped off the swing.

"What about Midsummer?" she asked hopefully. The Nazi army was too far away to march through the biggest celebration of the year. As she finished the question, a Soviet plane droned overhead.

"They're flying their planes out of the island bases." A glimmer sparked in Toomas's eyes. "We can't let the Soviets or the Nazis cancel our celebrations." His lips slanted into a grin. "I'll find you later. Mama and Papa are waiting for me."

It was easy to believe him. She nodded.

Valter hadn't waited for her. As Madli retrieved her bike, she looked back. The empty swing hung silent. Had it only been moments ago that she'd been laughing and flirting? How the world could change between heartbeats. An hour ago, the Germans were the enemy. Now, in a strange twist, they'd become hope for freedom.

The warmth of the sun freed the luxurious scent of grass and leaves. As she coasted along the crunchy gravel, the peaceful perfume of summer teased her. She wasn't in a hurry to get back and find out how complicated life was about to become.

When she got back to the farm, Valter's bicycle was leaning against the fence. Inside the house, she followed the staccato of static into the living room where Nana fiddled with the radio. Kalju, Grandpa, and Valter stood in front of the dining room table, arms crossed, ears ready. Peeter mimicked them. Madli sunk into the green velvet couch.

"Are we going to battle the Nazis now?" Peeter stood rigid. "I thought Estonia didn't want to fight."

"When the war started," Madli said, "Estonia told other countries it wanted to remain neutral. It's so small, though, that no one listened, or really cared."

"Where are the Nazi soldiers?" Peeter asked.

Madli shrugged. "We'll find out from the radio."

"If they came soon," Peeter said, "then Papa could come home."

If only it could be that easy. She held a finger to her lips as the static became a deep Russian voice.

"Turn up the volume," Grandpa commanded.

Madli leaned forward to catch each word. Maybe Peeter was right and the Nazis would advance rapidly. By some small miracle, Papa would come home, they'd celebrate her birthday together in October, and Christmas would be filled with presents. The frog would turn into a prince.

"Germany has attacked our country," the Russian voice stated. "Attacked our borders at many points and bombed from their airplanes our cites Zhitomir, Kiev, Sebastopol, Kaunas, and others, killing and wounding over two hundred persons. This attack upon our country is unparalleled in the history of civilized nations."

Kalju snorted. "Hah! You swine invaded the Baltics without any reason."

"Shhh!"

"Now that the attack on the Soviet Union has already been committed," the voice continued, "we have to order our men to drive the Nazi troops from the territory of our country. This war has been forced upon us by the clique of bloodthirsty Fascist rulers of Germany, who have already enslaved France, Czechoslovakia, Poland, Serbia, Norway, Belgium, Denmark, Holland, Greece, and other nations."

"He does have a point about the Nazis," Valter said. "They did begin the war."

Madli shrugged. The Soviets were giving the impression that the Nazi attack was unjustified and unprovoked.

Kalju shook his head. "The Soviets twist history to suit them."

"Hitler promised Stalin he wouldn't invade the Baltics," Grandpa said.

"Forbidden fruit is the most tempting," Nana said, fiddling

with the dial. "I'll try to find Helsinki or BBC London. They'll have something worthwhile."

After a couple spurts of static, a clipped English voice filled the room.

"What are they saying?" Nana asked Kalju.

"The Nazis have made rapid progress." Kalju's lips curled in the faintest hint of a smile. "Their army has more than three million men, three thousand tanks, and three thousand aircraft."

"Enough to bury the Russians?" Grandpa asked.

"The Soviet army is disorganized and full of young boys who can't ride bikes, much less organize an offensive," Kalju said.

Madli's toe traced the grey and burgundy flower on the carpet. Estonia was the monkey in the middle to the two most powerful armies in history.

Conversation ricocheted back and forth. Before long, talk between the boys and Grandpa changed to weapons, tanks, and aircraft. How many, how big, how many people each army could kill and whether it would be enough.

"Shhh." Madli leaned toward the radio to catch the last of the broadcast. New rules imposed by the Soviets. All vacationers must return to their places of work. A nine o'clock evening curfew. No bonfires.

No Midsummer.

A ridiculous, selfish question crossed Madli's mind: did the Nazis really need to invade on Jaanipäev? Shame heated her.

During the stubby, grey days of winter, with Papa in jail and Mama sobbing in the next room, Madli had heard the music of Midsummer night in her head and imagined the warmth of the bonfire. For months she'd lived for this party, to see Toomas, to dance on the midnight dew. Madli leaned back on the couch, arms crossed, legs crossed. The triple blow of the advancing Nazis, the order to return to Tallinn, and the cancelled Midsummer celebration made her feel like a child denied a birthday cake. It wasn't fair.

Nana turned off the radio. "No fire on the beach tonight."

Even Grandpa looked disappointed.

Valter nodded. "The Soviets will be flying planes out of their bases at the north end of the island. We wouldn't want them *accidentally* dropping bombs on us."

"The soldiers can't see through the walls," Nana said. "The party will be inside."

"We must have a bonfire," Peeter said. "Those evil spirits need to be scared away." His jaw jutted out.

Madli's stomach churned. "Nana, they said all vacationers are required to return to their places of work." She was barely able to spit the words out.

Nana shrugged. "We'll find out more." She turned off the radio. "Come and help me. Talk of war makes the men hungry."

"In a minute." The sight of food would make her heave. Madli stomped onto the veranda and plunked herself down onto the step. The desire to throw something caused her arm to jerk. Her feet itched to run through the woods, across the ocean. Far away. Her lungs begged to scream.

Instead, she seethed on the front porch. Pontu ambled over and nuzzled her leg with his cold nose. She scratched behind his ears.

Peeter sat down next to her. "Are the Nazis better than the Soviets?"

Madli shrugged. How could she answer that question in a way a seven-year-old would understand? Another plane droned overhead, followed by several more.

Peeter shivered. "Those planes are carrying bombs, aren't they?"

Madli draped her arm around his stiff shoulder. A real war had started. A war with guns and bombs and grenades. The last year of Soviet occupation had been one of arrests and deportations. Terrifying in a different way.

Nana thrust her head out the door. "Madli, come help with the meal. We can't build a bonfire, but we can eat and celebrate our health. We're the lucky ones."

Lucky ones, indeed. Papa in jail, Nazis on the doorstep, the Red Army in the trees.

They had to eat. They always had to eat. Madli trudged back into the kitchen. She mixed together rye, oats, barley, and pease-meal flour in a large bowl to make *kamakäkk*. With a thump, she pummelled the mixture into a smooth consistency and rolled it into little balls.

Perhaps the Nazis would save them.

She set the *sõir* on the table. The soft cheese with caraway seeds was one of her favourites.

Maybe the Soviets would retreat.

She laid out more bread and homemade beer with honey. A whiff of the delicious smell of *shashlõkk* wafted into the kitchen from the outside grill. She was one of the lucky ones.

Maybe Toomas would come tonight.

For the first time, the Midsummer supper was eaten inside with the curtains drawn and the radio in the background. Madli's mood matched the dim light of the room. Any chance of Toomas slinking through the forest evaporated.

"*Jätku leiba.*" Grandpa raised a glass of beer at the start of the meal.

"Winston Churchill called Hitler a 'bloodthirsty guttersnipe' and pledged Britain's help for the Soviet Union in any way possible." Kalju's smirk broke over his face.

Madli tucked her elbows in, as Valter on one side of her and Kalju on the other both reached across the table for the beer, the bread, and the potatoes. She picked at her food.

"Potatoes, please." Grandpa stretched out his hand. "Not sure what a 'guttersnipe' is, but it sounds about right."

As the honey beer flowed, the conversation grew heated. "The Soviets have achieved the unthinkable. They've made us want to welcome the Nazis. For hundreds of years we've despised the German lords in their fancy manor houses, making life miserable for Estonian peasants as we shovelled their manure," Kalju said.

"The Germans weren't the only ones. Russians, Swedes, Danes. There were countless invaders. In spite of them all, we've survived. With our language, our food, and our customs. *Tervist*!" Grandpa raised a tankard of beer, chugged it down, and drew his sleeve across his mouth.

It was a halfhearted attempt to celebrate without the bonfire, the sea, and the light of the longest day of the year. The talk of war bored her. Opinions volleyed back and forth. The Soviets would retreat with their tails between their legs. The Nazis would rescue them from the evil Soviet toads. The Estonians would conquer the world. And she'd become queen of the Baltics.

As she cleaned the table Madli wiped the crumbs toward her, following an old superstition. If she wiped the crumbs the other way, all the good fortune would be swept out of the house. A daft custom, but Nana would notice.

The evening stretched interminably. Every few minutes, Madli would excuse herself to the kitchen to peer out the window. By ten o'clock she knew Toomas wouldn't arrive.

"Come, play the piano again." Valter's eyes were dark and bottomless. He reached for her hand.

Valter had been in a snit all afternoon, barely exchanging a word with her. A few beers later, he was back to flirting.

Another time his smile would have charmed her. Madli tucked her hand behind her back. "I have to wash the dishes." She ignored the flash of annoyance in his eyes.

Dishes clattered as Madli filled the sink with soapy water. Alone in the kitchen, she scrubbed the plates clean and set them in the rack to dry. Elbow deep in soapy water, she was washing a glass when hands gripped her shoulders. Hands that burned through her blouse.

Madli didn't drop the glass, though all sensation drained from her fingers.

"Let's see if we can find a blooming fern," Toomas whispered in her ear. "Sorry, I tried to come sooner, but my parents couldn't stop talking about the invasion. Come on, let's go."

His breath tickled her neck. She didn't dare move for fear his hands would vanish.

The air felt as thick as sauna heat. Madli peered over her left shoulder into blue eyes, inches away. Warmth crept into her cheeks. "I'll meet you outside." A few more glasses left to wash. "In a couple of minutes."

Strong hands squeezed her shoulders. "I'll wait outside." The door shut with a bang.

Madli managed to draw air into her lungs. A smile crept onto her lips.

The rest of the glasses received a hasty wipe and rinse. "Good enough," she muttered. She dried her hands and smoothed her hair. Did she need a sweater? Didn't matter. She flung the towel on a hook and bumped into a muscular chest that didn't belong to Toomas.

"Where's the beer? Are you coming back to the living room?" Valter's eyes pierced hers. "Is the talk of war boring you?"

"Um ... I ..." Madli was speechless. She found her hands on his chest, to push him away.

Valter's hand tucked under her elbow. "Let's go for a walk and search for blooming ferns," he whispered in a low voice.

The intensity of his gaze ignited a thought. Could Valter have a romantic interest in her? Kalju had teased her about Valter being a "fine young man," but Madli considered him a cousin. Tonight his firm grip on her elbow hinted otherwise, as did his quest to find ferns. Her feet anchored themselves to the floor. "I need to finish cleaning the dishes."

"Dishes can wait," Valter said.

Short of grabbing the sink and hanging on, there was nothing she could do to resist. Madli let him propel her toward the door. Panic took root in her stomach and spread. She sidestepped into the pantry. "I can't go right now." No believable excuse came to mind.

"Why not?" An attractive pout passed over Valter's lips.

Before she could reply, the door opened.

"Coming?" Toomas peered around the doorframe. "Hello, Valter." He retreated outside.

The screen door slammed.

For the second time in the day, Valter's face smoothed into a mask. He nodded. "Back to the dirty dishes." Stiff-shouldered, he walked back to the living room.

Madli lingered in the pantry. She was no expert with boys but his attention since her arrival, his vague disapproval of Toomas at the swing, his closeness when they sat together on the piano bench indicated he liked her.

Her fingers swept back her hair. She licked her lips and wiped her damp palms on her skirt.

Madli slid out the door onto the porch and scanned the lawn. Where did Toomas go? The lavender light cast long shadows and it took a moment to detect him. He leaned against the birch tree by the storage barn.

By the time Madli had crossed the lawn, her smile was a beacon. "So where can we find those ferns?" Madli relaxed her smile. Too eager, she thought.

"In the forest, well away from the light."

His deep voice was velvet in the dark.

"Come, hold my hand in case you stumble," he said.

Madli slipped her hand into his warm grip. He gave it a squeeze and her heart skipped a beat.

They entered the grey darkness of the forest. The scent was different in the cool of the night. Moist and fresh with earth.

Each step snapped twigs and crackled leaves.

Madli struggled for conversation. "What will happen to us? Us Estonians," she clarified.

"Over here." Toomas pulled her toward him. "Let's sit on the big rock."

Madli sat down and Toomas settled beside her. The length of his thigh burned alongside hers. The last quarter moon peeked through the branches. She could barely breathe.

Toomas fumbled in his pocket and pulled out tobacco and a tin of paper. He licked the edge of the paper, tucked a couple pinches of tobacco inside, and rolled it up. With the cigarette dangling from his lips, he lit it with a steady, practised movement. His head tilted back as he took a long drag.

As he exhaled, the acrid smell tickled her nose.

"Remember the story of *Kaval Ants ja Vanapagan*?" Toomas gazed up at the sky.

"Of course. Clever Hans was the servant who constantly outwitted his old master, the Devil." Discussing a fairy tale wasn't the romantic conversation Madli had in mind.

"We want to be like Hans. Cunning and smart. We'll never outnumber the enemy, so we'll need to outsmart him." Toomas took another puff. "Fortunately, that's not hard."

Talk of war was tedious but she'd listen if it kept him interested. "How will we do that?" His profile carved out of the evening light etched itself into her memory. She memorized the angle of his lean fingers curled around the thin cigarette.

"By luring them onto our ground and fighting on our terms. In the forest, where we've fought our battles for hundreds of years." The tip of the cigarette burned orange. "The Forest Brothers are gaining strength against the Soviets. They don't have the numbers to attack them in an open field, but can ambush them in the woods."

"Who would join the Forest Brothers?" Madli remembered the men with their families in the woods.

"I would, for one," Toomas said. "This forest is as familiar as my house. Plus, I'm a crack shot."

"And your parents?" Madli wanted to grab the words as they floated out of her mouth.

Toomas shook his head. "They wouldn't approve." His cigarette trembled. He dragged a last puff, flicked it onto the rock and crushed it with his shoe.

Slowly he turned toward her.

Madli's heart fluttered. He was going to kiss her. *Issand Jumal.* What if their lips missed?

Toomas leaned in. Both eyes were closed.

Madli met him halfway, eyes parted slightly to ensure they didn't bump noses.

His lips landed on hers. Warm, smoky full lips. Her eyes shut. The kiss didn't last nearly long enough. "I hope we're not Koit and Hämarik, fated to kiss only on Midsummer night." Madli took a deep breath.

"Ah, yes. That poor unfortunate couple. They kissed ever so briefly once a year." Toomas tightened his arm around her waist. "It would be bad luck to kiss once." His fingers guided her face to his.

This time both her eyes closed. The rock melted away. Time dissolved.

"I kept all your letters," Toomas said afterward, his arm draped across her shoulder.

"I kept both of yours." Madli traced the scar on his chin with her finger.

"This scar is your fault." Toomas stroked her hand. His face melted into a smile. "I was five."

Twigs rustled. Madli stiffened. "There's someone in the forest."

"Animals." His arms wrapped around her.

"I think it's a person," she said.

"As long as it's one person." He guided her hand around his neck. "Not an army."

Her other hand scooped the back of his head to draw his lips to hers. Electricity charged through her.

Hours later, after saying goodbye to Toomas, Madli floated back to her room. She perched on the edge of the bed and buried her nose in the daisies and cornflowers Toomas had picked. Gently, she tucked them under her pillow. Sweet dreams. *Head und.*

Her mittens went on like armour. As she lay on the pillow and pulled the covers up to her nose, the woollen scent comforted her. "Magic mittens, cast a spell," she whispered to the mittens, to God, to anything else that might contain magic.

Tuesday, June 22, 1941

Kallis Papa,

We hope for freedom from the strangest corner of the world.
The Nazis. They invaded the Soviet Union today. At least
the Nazis celebrate Christmas, so we can have presents,
kringel, and a tree.

   Perhaps it's a good thing, but why today? Jaanipäev.
My favourite celebration. There was no party, no bonfire on
the beach, no dancing. You would have been disappointed as
well. It's so shallow, but am I awful to want a few minutes
of joy?

   I hate war. I just want my life back. It's petty, given
how many people are suffering, but it's true. I know you'd
understand.

   Soon, Papa, soon.

CHAPTER TWELVE

On Tuesday morning, Madli's scissors snipped angrily. She was cutting material for heavy blackout curtains, necessary so that planes wouldn't find them at night. There'd been no sign of Toomas since Jaanipäev. Two days ago. The flowers under her pillow had wilted along with her hopes. Valter avoided her. Boys were impossible.

Her summer vacation was over. The Soviets demanded that all vacationers return to their home towns. In a few days she'd take the boat back to the mainland. The scissors slid along the kitchen table, chopping the fabric.

Gravel crunched in the front yard. Footsteps pounded up the porch stairs. She peeked out the window. Toomas. Finally. Snip, snip, snip along the black fabric. A grin curled her lips, but she straightened it into a frown. Her heart thumped faster and faster.

Toomas peered in the window. "Hi, Madli."

"I'm in the kitchen," she said. Of course, he could see that. Her scissors plunked onto the table as Toomas walked in. His shirt was stained with sweat and his hands were grimy with dirt. Without a word, he headed directly to the water jug, poured a glass, and chugged it down.

He sat down at the kitchen table opposite her. For a moment he gazed at her, then smiled as though he remembered their kiss.

Heat dotted her cheeks. "I'm making blackout shields for the window." Another obvious statement.

"Where is everyone?" Toomas wiped his brow. "It's awfully quiet."

"Grandpa and the boys are staking the open fields," Madli answered. "The island will look like a porcupine with wooden bristles."

The Soviets had ordered the residents to protect the island from the Nazis. Every flat open space, every meadow, every field, pasture, and farmyard had to be staked by posts two metres high and sharpened to a point. The posts were placed at four-metre intervals so that Nazi parachuters couldn't land in the open areas.

Toomas nodded. "Can't miss those stakes in the yard." He picked his damp shirt away from his body. "I've been digging on the beach." He saluted. "I obey the Red Army."

"The Soviets are forcing us to build our own prison," Madli said, her throat tight. "The Nazis can't land on the island."

"They'll think of another way." His lips drew into a line. "We dug long troughs up and down the beach. If a Nazi plane tries to land on the sand, its wheels will dip into our fine ditches and it'll topple over, crash and burn."

Hopeless.

Toomas reached across the table for her hand. "What can we do?"

It was more a statement than a question. Answers flew through her mind. Run, escape, hide. Pray. Dream. Hope.

"*Püsime edasi*," he said. We carry on.

Madli heaved a sigh. There were no answers.

"I must get back." Toomas stood up.

Madli stood up and took a step toward him. He raised his arms, but she was already there, her arms clasped around his waist, cheek against his damp shirt. She needed one tiny moment of magic.

They stood entwined. Finally, she lifted her head. She didn't open her eyes, just found his lips and the world disappeared.

As he rode away on his bicycle, she touched her lips. It had been only a moment, but it was enough.

❖

The radio sustained them as its words fed them hope. Grandpa drank his tea beside the radio, ate lunch next to it, and sat beside it in the evening until he went to bed.

Each day the Nazi army pushed closer to Estonia. Each day the Soviets panicked more. The Soviets would confiscate horses, wagons, cars, and bikes. No doubt to make sure Nazi parachutists couldn't hop on a bicycle and conquer the Red Army.

Nana baked. "We need bread." Breadmaking kept Nana going as she pounded, kneaded, and thumped the dough, as she wiped sweat from her brow and washed flour off her hands.

On Wednesday, Grandpa couldn't leave the radio. Finland had announced they were at war with the USSR. "Madli, take some food to our friends in the forest," he said.

"Today?" Constant drizzle had turned everything a midsummer emerald.

"They're counting on us," Grandpa said. "They're damp and hungry." He glanced around the comfortable room. "Nana, pack some food so Madli can take it to the families hiding in the forest."

Why couldn't the boys fetch and carry? Madli was already tired of this newborn war, only two days old. She dragged herself off the green velvet couch, found a sweater and raincoat. Nana offered her a bag of supplies and Madli stepped out into a grey day. Her toes squished wet leather.

In the shelter of the forest, the rain merely dripped. Thick silence was broken by the hum of thousands of ravenous mosquitoes. Madli snapped off a branch to fend them away. She approached the camp flailing wildly.

"Who are you?" The voice came from behind a large tree.

A surge of fear bolted her feet to the ground. Madli clutched the bag of food as a shield. Immediately, the bloodthirsty mosquitoes attacked her. She flapped her branch an attempt to get rid of them.

"Don't move," came the command. The unmistakable click of a rifle bolt halted her.

"It's the mosquitoes," Madli pleaded. "They're attacking me."

A rifle barrel slid out from behind the tree trunk. An arm in a brown shirt followed.

Madli flapped her arms to get rid of the bugs. "I'm Arvo's granddaughter. I'm bringing food to the camp." She held out the linen bag as proof.

The arm holding the rifle belonged to a young man with a fuzzy growth of brown beard. A frown creased his otherwise smooth forehead. His gaze fixed over her shoulder. "Who's he?"

"Who?" Madli brushed a mosquito off her cheek.

"Him. Behind you."

Madli swung around. She couldn't believe her eyes. Valter stood pink-faced, dark hair slick with rain and his hands hanging guiltily by his side. "Valter? What are you doing here?" He'd avoided her the last couple of days.

"I thought you went for a walk in the forest. I was going to catch up to you." Valter shrugged his shoulders.

"Why?" Madli swatted her legs. Why didn't the mosquitoes attack Valter instead?

"Who's he?" the man asked again, rifle fixed on Valter.

"Valter lives with Grandpa," Madli said. "I mean Arvo."

"What's your name?" The rifle pointed at Valter.

"Valter."

"Valter what?"

"Novikov," he whispered.

"*Kurat*," the man swore. "A Russian, eh?" The rifle trembled. His eyes darted to Madli. "He forced you to come here, didn't he?"

"No." Good God. The man considered Valter a Russian spy. "Of course not." Madli waved her hand as the man fixed the rifle on Valter. "Listen to me! Where's Jaan? He knows me and Grandpa. He'll tell you." Sheer panic fired her burst of authority.

At the mention of Jaan's name, the man swung the rifle toward the camp. "All right. Both of you, let's go."

Madli glared at Valter, but he gazed straight ahead.

At the camp, no women and children were visible this time. Instead, several men constructed a shelter out of branches and foliage. Four giant beehive structures had already been built. Each had a small low door covered with a tarp.

"Hey, Jaan," the man shouted. "Come here."

The lean man with the tousled blond hair put down his axe and came toward them.

"Madli," Jaan said. His tired smile caused the lines in his face to deepen. "Who's your friend?" He shoved the muzzle of the man's rifle toward the ground. "We don't need this. Thank you Mikk, you did a fine job and can go back to your sentry post. I'll talk to them."

"He's a Russian," Mikk said. With a final suspicious glance, he headed back to his guard duties. "There may be more spies who followed him here."

"Valter lives with Grandpa." Madli's voice and gaze were steady. "His father was Russian. Both of his parents died in a farming accident years ago. They worked for Grandpa, so he took care of Valter afterward."

Valter crossed his arms.

"Why haven't we met him before?"

Madli shrugged and changed the subject. "I brought bread and new potatoes and fish. And beer, too."

"*Suur aitah*," Jaan said in thanks. "Arvo is a good man." He confronted Valter. "Are you going to join us?"

"Join you?" Valter asked. A quick twitch of his brow indicated his puzzlement.

"The Forest Brothers. To fight for Estonia's freedom." Jaan's gaze was steady as Valter shrugged his shoulders. "And why not? Which side are you on?"

Madli remembered Nana's words about trusting no one.

"How will you fight without weapons, or equipment, or radios?" Valter asked.

"So you have conditions?" Jaan's voice tensed. "Patriotism isn't enough? You'll pick the side better armed?"

A change of subject was in order. "Grandpa — Arvo," Madli corrected herself, "said to tell you that Finland has declared war on the USSR."

Jaan nodded, his eyes evaluating Valter. "Tell your grandfather we're recruiting."

"Recruiting?" Madli asked. A dozen men working in the clearing. A couple of foliage shelters. Laundry strung between two trees. Hardly the makings of an army.

"For the Forest Brothers," Jaan said, blue eyes intense with conviction. "If you support the Nazis, the Soviets will kill you. If you support the Soviets, the Nazis will kill you. So we're fighting for ourselves and our country." He waved his hand toward the small group of men. "If you know anyone who wants to fight for Estonia, come tell me first. Our location must remain secret." His gaze dropped over Valter. "We need to make sure we can trust them."

Madli nodded. "I understand." A surge of pride coursed through her. With nothing more than patriotism and a few weapons, they would fight and expect to win. A drop in the ocean that would ripple across the miles.

Or be washed away in the waves.

Madli and Valter walked back through the forest. Rain dribbled down her neck as she waited for Valter to say something. Tempted to swat him, she finally asked, "Why did you follow me?"

"I wanted to talk to you," Valter mumbled. "Alone. Instead I get confronted by twenty guys in a forest deluding themselves they can beat both the Soviets and the Nazis. They have no chance, not even with lots of enthusiasm and enough vodka."

"The Forest Brothers are patriots." An uneasy feeling simmered in her stomach.

"They won't stand a chance against the two most powerful armies in history," Valter growled. "You're putting yourself in danger by associating with them. And him."

He meant Toomas. "Hardly," Madli said to spite Valter, but her stomach churned. He was right. For the Soviets, a whiff of dissent was enough to warrant a knock on the door in the middle of the night.

Valter stepped in front of her. The intensity from his eyes radiated conviction. "The Soviets know who's loyal and who's not."

"That's what you wanted to tell me?" Madli asked. "'Be careful'?" She sidestepped Valter, sweeping her branch through the air. "With my lifelong friends?" Madli strode back to the farm, heart pounding with each step, while the rain washed away her certainty.

Wednesday, June 25, 1941

Kallis Papa,

I don't know whether to pity the Forest Brothers or admire them. What can one person do? How can twenty people or two hundred or even two thousand people with only hope and determination, and perhaps the occasional functional rifle, battle against three million men with marching boots?

People fear the Soviets more than the devil. Any hint of partisan opinion, any trace of disloyalty is reason for arrest. I fear for Toomas, for anyone who fights for Estonia.

I don't want to be scared to see my friends. But I am.

I don't want to be bullied into submission. But I will succumb.

Because I want to live. To see you and Mama. To be together on my birthday, eating kringel, drinking coffee, and singing.

If you were here, you'd tell me, "The pen is mightier than the sword."

One person, one book, one pen could make a difference.

If the time were right. If anyone were listening.

CHAPTER THIRTEEN

The Soviets know who's loyal and who's not.

Over the next couple of days, Valter's words haunted her as the Red Army formed destruction battalions. The hordes attracted men with shady motives. Men who wanted to settle personal scores with the weight of the Red Army behind them.

Nana's words from the sauna echoed in Madli's mind. Power. Not wanting to be on the losing side. How addictive power would be to young men with little education and a weakness for violence.

Late Saturday night, Madli walked hand in hand with Toomas through the woods. A sliver of moon cast a grey light.

They settled on a big rock in the forest.

Madli snuggled close to him, but didn't let herself melt. Valter was right. Toomas was a target for arrest. For the last two days she'd ached to see him, but was afraid he'd be dragged off off by the Soviet army. Arrested. Shot. Killed.

And she'd be associated with someone guilty of patriotism. Again.

"What's wrong?" Toomas asked.

"Nothing." She folded her hands in her lap.

Toomas took a breath as if to ask a question, but exhaled with pursed lips.

"I'm tired," Madli said. Tired of Soviets, tired of war, tired of thinking each day might be the day she'd lose him. Or Kalju. Or Grandpa, or Valter.

Papa had always encouraged her to speak her mind. "Toomas," Madli began.

"Yes."

As his lips nuzzled her neck, all thought evaporated. She'd speak her mind after the kiss.

It took her a moment to remember her question.

"Have you ever thought of hiding in the woods?" Madli whispered into his shoulder.

"I can't do that," Toomas said.

His muscles tensed. He pulled back.

Panic welled. "Why not? You're a target for the destruction battalions."

Toomas shook his head.

"Why are you so dense?" His stubbornness ignited a bonfire in her. "War is stupid." Madli threw down the verbal gauntlet. In the dimness of the woods, the words hung in the air.

"Our country, our freedom, and our integrity are not stupid." Toomas spat out the last word.

"Dying needlessly is," Madli retorted. "You can't fight if you're arrested."

"Whose side are you on?"

"Yours," Madli said. "Ours."

"Doesn't sound like it." Toomas snapped open his tin of paper, peeled off a leaf, and stuffed it with tobacco.

Madli's heart dropped. She'd gone too far. She'd picked a battle for no reason other than that she was scared.

"Of course I'm on our side," she said more calmly. "I couldn't be anything else. Papa believed in our freedom."

"You have your own mind." Toomas took a drag of his cigarette. "What do you believe?"

Madli wasn't sure if she could tease apart her own opinion. Her thoughts were entwined with Papa's ideas. But she had to say something; otherwise Toomas would think she was vapid.

"I have his manuscript," she blurted out. "I took it from his office the night he was arrested. If I didn't believe in freedom for Estonia, why would I risk my life?" She took a deep breath. "When Papa returns, the world will know the truth."

"What are you talking about?" Toomas asked slowly.

Madli explained that her father had written a history of Estonia. It went into detail about the country's independence from Germany after World War I, its success as an independent republic in the last twenty years, and the terror of the early Soviet occupation. Her voice dropped to a whisper. "He believes there's a secret clause in the non-agression pact signed by the Nazis and Soviets."

"What do you mean?" Toomas breathed out the words.

"Hitler and Stalin agreed to divide the Baltic States, Finland, Romania, and Poland into spheres of influence. The Soviet Union got the Baltics. Hitler got Poland." When she had first read it, it was incomprehensible that their country had been given away. What right did anyone have to bargain with an independent nation?

For a moment, Toomas didn't take a breath. The ash from

his cigarette smouldered. "So it's true." His shoulders slumped. "There have been rumours." He sat straighter. "It doesn't really change anything for us right now. Where's the document?"

"Under my mattress."

The cigarette froze halfway to his lips. "Does anyone know?" Madli shook her head. Her chest was tight.

The cigarette continued to his lips. Smoke drifted out of his nose and mouth.

"And you're worried about *me*?" Toomas snorted.

"No." The word fell out her mouth in self-defence.

The cigarette glowed red. He pulled it out of his mouth and crushed it with his foot. "Oh."

Saturday, June 28, 1941

Kallis Papa,

On June 26th, the Nazis took Daugavpils, the southeast corner of Latvia.

The bad news now is that the Soviets are forming destruction battalions. These so-called People's Defence Units justify killing anyone who doesn't support the Soviets. Nana calls them thugs who couldn't defend a chicken coop. Grandpa calls them something much worse.

More people have taken to the woods. Is hiding cowardice or just smart? You can't fight from the back of a wagon with Soviet soldiers watching your every move.

Would I die for my country? For my beliefs? Or would I hide?

I never said I was sorry for the quarrel we had the night before you were arrested. I did the same thing today with Toomas. My temper flared like a juniper's flame because I'm scared for his safety. I argued like an old fishwoman. He was offended when I suggested he hide in the forest. Then he left.

I'm sorry, Papa. I never got the chance to say I'm sorry before they arrested you.

You have to come back.

I need to say I'm sorry.

Late Tuesday night Madli sat in bed by the window and wrote in her diary. The lamp on the bedside table cast a grey light. A quiet tap at the door startled her.

"Toomas?" she whispered, hopeful. Two days had gone by since she'd seen him. Pride prevented her from making amends, but her heart ached with both shame and regret.

Kalju peered around the door. He entered and sat on the small wooden chair beside her bed, legs stretched out, arms folded across his chest. "What should I do?" His lips twisted in deliberation. The last couple of weeks at the farm had suited her brother. Tanned and healthy, his cheeks had filled out and his brown hair had lightened.

"Do?" Madli didn't understand. Kalju never asked for advice. Part of being the oldest meant he knew it all. Or pretended to.

"Do. As in fight. Pick sides." His eyes reflected anguish. "But I can't desert you and Peeter." Slim fingers twisted the buttons on his shirt.

The pencil slipped through her fingers.

No. Kalju dying on a lonely, cold battlefield.

No. How could she tell Mama that her oldest son, her favourite, her hope for the future, had been killed?

Patriotism was one thing.

Dying for it another.

"Hide." It wasn't a patriotic reaction, only a sister trying to save her brother. "What would I tell Mama?" A too-familiar lump swelled in her throat. "Or Papa."

"Hiding is a coward's choice." A thin grin tightened Kalju's lips. "Papa didn't raise cowards, either in action or in speech." He shrugged. "Though it would be difficult to explain helping the Nazi army."

"Papa would be horrified." His words had hit her like a hammer, but Madli couldn't get teary-eyed and emotional. Kalju responded to logic. She adopted her most persuasive tone. "We finally got rid of the Germans less than twenty-five years ago. Papa devoted his life to exposing the rise of the Nazis and the brutality of the Soviets."

"And now to actually welcome them back with open arms." Kalju stretched his arms over his head. "Blasphemous, that's what it is."

"Yes." She hoped he would heed his own words. "Papa wanted democracy. Hitler and Stalin want power. Papa would under-stand if you didn't side with either." At least a coward would be alive, she thought. Bravery was overrated.

"So my option is to join the Forest Brothers?" Kalju pursed his lips and exhaled. "What are they using for weapons? Soup spoons and sauna ladles?"

Madli's lips twitched; tears welled despite her resolve not to cry. "You can't go." A sob broke through. She couldn't keep the manuscript a secret any longer. "I have to tell you something. Papa and I had an argument the night before his arrest. He's gone and I can't tell him how sorry I am. It was so stupid. He wanted me to go back to school to be a teacher. And I told him I couldn't teach in the Soviet system. He only wanted the best for me and saw a future where the Soviets were gone. I couldn't see that." Tears gushed down her face. "I went back the night he was arrested. I saw the soldiers take him away."

She felt Kalju's astonishment.

In her mind's eye, she travelled back to the dark street on that cold November night. "I went by the office on my way home. I knew he was going out to dinner. As I approached the building, three men came out. Two soldiers and Papa."

"Why were you there?" Kalju's jaw dropped.

"To apologize." Madli smeared tears over her cheeks.

She had hid in the shadows of the building, the cold stone like a block of ice against her back. Terror grabbed her heart and squeezed. In the dim light, she wouldn't allow herself to believe it was Papa. His posture was military — no doubt from his time in the army during the War of Independence. She wanted to run to him, grab the heavy wool of his dark overcoat, but knew that it would be futile. The soldiers had pushed him into a black car.

"He never saw me," Madli whispered. "He never heard me say I'm sorry."

He'd never kiss the tip of her nose. Or tweak her cheeks.

"Don't go." Eyes puffy, she appealed to Kalju.

Kalju sat beside her on the bed. His arms enveloped her. "It's a terrible time with terrible choices."

After he left, Madli sat in her dimly lit room, holding her pencil. Kalju fighting for the Nazis. Unthinkable only days ago. What would she do to regain control over her life? Her pencil became a pistol and her finger curved around an imaginary trigger. Could she? Would she?

Tuesday, July 1, 1941

Kallis Papa,

It's too dangerous to travel now. The Nazis are advancing

more rapidly than anyone expected. We won't return to Tallinn until it is safe. That's the only good news.

Kalju wants to be patriotic and struggles with a terrible choice. Should he aid the Nazis? He's afraid joining them will disappoint you. It would disappoint me. I hope he'll realize that hiding in the woods is a better option. One that will keep him alive.

We all want our freedom back. What price will we pay?

CHAPTER FOURTEEN

On Thursday morning, Madli pummelled bread dough. The men had taken to the fields early to harvest the hay. Nana and Peeter weeded the vegetable garden in the back. Madli was stuck in the kitchen on a glorious summer day making bread and sewing rags.

Deep fist marks created cavities in the dough. She forced the dough into four loaves.

Toomas hadn't stopped by since Sunday. She'd obviously done a great job of convincing him she wasn't interested. At least she'd done that well.

Tears burned. She wouldn't cry. She hadn't meant anything she'd said. She couldn't stand the thought of him arrested. Now he thought she didn't care.

Madli tossed the loaves into the oven.

She returned to the kitchen table to cut up old pillowcases

and towels to make pads for her monthlies. A pot full of old cloths bubbled on the stove. After she finished cutting, she sewed. She folded the fabric into four, pumped the pedal on the Singer sewing machine, and created a neat border around the rectangular pad. The needle whirred along the fabric as she pumped the pedal harder. The rhythm soothed her frayed nerves.

Later in the day she would go to Toomas. She would find the words to apologize.

The scent of freshly baked bread wafted through the room. The radio blared marching tunes, endless Soviet propaganda about the strength of the Motherland and the stalwart commitment of the people as they rallied against the Nazi advance. Never mind that the Nazis were getting closer by the day. The sound of the Russian language annoyed her. It was guttural, harsh, thick like a winter stew. It didn't have the clear sing-song quality of Estonian.

Outside, a car door slammed. Madli's foot froze on the sewing pedal. Soldiers never travelled alone. Sure enough, a second door slammed. She threw her sweater on top of her pile of rags and rushed to the window overlooking the drive. With a trembling hand she drew the curtain back to peer out. Two young Soviet soldiers, one tall and the other with blond hair, advanced to the porch. They were carrying rifles.

By the time they arrived at the door, she couldn't tell the difference between their knocking and the thumping of her heart. Madli's feet wanted to run, but bullets travelled faster than feet. She wiped her damp hands on her skirt and twisted the doorknob.

The soldiers filled the doorway. The blond wore a crumpled shirt, and the tall soldier's collar was stained with sweat. Crumpled Shirt's hair was plastered to his head. Exhaustion etched their faces and for one foolish moment she felt sorry for them.

The memory of Sarah smiling at the soldiers on the street flashed through her mind. Soviet flies.

"Yes?" Madli bestowed what she hoped passed for a warm smile and not a grimace. Valter said her mouth twisted at the corners when she lied. These soldiers wouldn't know that.

Neither soldier mirrored her smile.

They didn't shoot her either.

Small blessings.

"Who else is home?" Sweaty Collar peered into the house. "You're not alone, are you?"

"Grandpa and Valter are in the hay field," she replied. "Nana is weeding the garden out back." Close enough to hear her if she screamed.

Maybe.

"Peeter, my younger brother, is with Nana." She didn't mention Kalju.

Sweaty Collar took a deep breath and his eyes closed for a millisecond. A distant, rapturous expression swept away the lines on his face. He took another deep breath as his tongue glided over his lips and moaned slightly as he exhaled.

His bizarre behaviour mesmerized her until she took another breath. The scent of freshly baked bread made her taste buds scream for a slice. Bread might be a better weapon than a gun or grenade. "Would you like some fresh bread?" Her teeth bared in a reasonable copy of a smile. "And milk?" The memory of Sarah tossing her head when she flirted with the soldiers on the street came back to her. Madli attempted an awkward hair flip.

Crumpled Shirt's blue eyes widened as he nodded. "*Da.*"

The appearance of youth still lingered in his face. Before long, however, the softness would vanish and be replaced by harsh angles. An odour of rank sweat hit her nostrils. Didn't Soviet soldiers ever bathe? She didn't ask their reason for coming here.

If the soldiers intended to deport her family, they wouldn't take time to eat and drink, would they?

"Come into the kitchen." Madli led the way to the table. "I'll get glasses and plates." The army had taken their quota of food from the farm, and it annoyed her to share more with them.

The aroma of fresh bread hypnotized the soldiers. They rested their rifles against the wall and plunked themselves down onto the kitchen chairs, forearms resting on the table. Like pigs gathered around the trough at mealtime. No sooner had she placed two glasses of milk and a plate of bread on the table than the food was gone. Both wiped their shirtsleeves across their mouths, as her brothers would do.

"More?" Madli asked, sure of the answer. She prayed they wouldn't fill her with bullets after filling their stomachs.

They nodded. "*Spaseebo.*" An entire loaf of bread later, Crumpled Shirt finally spoke. "We are here to take your bicycles and radio," he said. "Weapons. Knives, daggers, pistols, shovels." An apologetic tone crept into his voice.

It was common knowledge that the army would confiscate all radios, bicycles, and weapons. All were registered, so lying was pointless.

"Of course," Madli said, weak with relief that it was objects, not people, they had come to round up. She cleared the plates and glasses. As she passed by the stove she stirred the rags, blushing when she remembered the contents of the pot.

"Do you have women in your army?" The question popped out of her mouth.

Crumpled Shirt's eyebrows shot up. He nodded. "My sister is in the army. It's no place for a woman."

"Shhh." Sweaty Collar put a finger to his lips. "Listen. Stalin is going to speak." He headed toward the living room.

After a second of confusion, Madli's ears tuned in to the radio.

The announcer, excited and stumbling over his words, repeated that Stalin would speak in a couple of minutes.

"We must listen." Crumpled Shirt headed toward the living room.

Madli scrambled to join them. How dare they waltz into the living room with their dirty boots on?

The soldiers stood in front of the radio in Grandpa's living room. When the announcer breathlessly introduced their leader, Crumpled Shirt's eyes shifted and his shoulders levelled as he stood up straighter. The posture of a soldier who revered his commander-in-chief. "Our Great Leader." His voice was hushed. "He hasn't spoken on the radio since 1938. This is the second time in history."

A coarse voice cut through the air like a threshing machine. "Comrades. Citizens. Brothers and sisters. I am addressing you, my friends."

For Madli, Stalin was a picture on the wall, a poster in every school and public building. A cruel face with slick black hair, a caterpillar moustache, and insect eyes. The force behind the ideology that had arrested her father, made them move from their home, and deported hundreds of people. She'd never considered him a real person. Goosebumps popped up on her arms. Shivers cascaded up and down her spine.

He was real.

The war was real.

"Hitler's troops have succeeded in capturing Lithuania, a considerable part of Latvia, the western part of Byelo-Russia, part of Western Ukraine."

All in the span of two weeks. Madli smiled. She chewed the side of her finger.

"There must be no room in our ranks for whimperers and cowards, for panic-mongers and deserters," Stalin continued.

"We must exterminate spies, diversionists, and enemy parachut-ists. In case of forced retreat of Red Army units, all rolling stock must be evacuated. The enemy must not be left a single engine, a single railway car, not a single pound of grain or a gallon of fuel."

A gasp escaped her mouth. He wanted to destroy them all.

"In areas occupied by the enemy, guerrilla units must be formed, diversionist groups must be organized to combat the enemy troops, to blow up bridges and roads, damage telephone and telegraph lines, set fire to forests, stores, transports. In the occupied regions conditions must be made unbearable for the enemy and all his accomplices."

Fear settled in her heart and bolted down.

"Forward to our victory." Stalin ended his speech.

Crumpled Shirt drew his hand up in a slow salute. Sweaty Collar did the same.

"It's an honour to serve the Motherland." The words nearly gagged her. "I'm so glad we had the radio to hear Stalin. It'll be a shame to lose it."

"We must obey orders," Crumpled Shirt said with a faraway gaze in his eye. A new authority energized him.

"I'll show you where the bicycles are in the shed. You know where the radio is." Madli laughed nervously. "I'll find Grandpa and he'll get the weapons for you."

"One more thing." He pulled papers from his pocket. "Here is a conscription notice for Valter Novikov. Any male eighteen and older is required to report to Heltermaa Harbour tomorrow by two o'clock."

Madli's heart pounded. "For what?"

"For the Soviet army. To defend the Motherland against the Nazi vermin." He handed her a paper. "Are there other men here born between 1918 and 1921?"

"No." The lie slipped out easily. Her eyes kept his gaze.

"Make certain this Valter shows up," Crumpled Shirt said. "Otherwise, we'll come find him. And you."

Her breath caught.

She shouldn't have wasted a loaf of bread. *Kurat*. Poor Valter.

The paper fluttered in her trembling hand as she placed it on the kitchen table. The soldiers grabbed their rifles and followed her out of the house. She pointed them toward the shed, then raced over to the vegetable garden where Nana and Peeter weeded tomatoes and cucumbers.

One thought careened through her mind: to save Kalju from conscription, she had lied to the Soviet army.

⬦

The distance from the house to the vegetable garden was a stone's throw, but when she arrived she was gasping raggedly. Nana's blue kerchief bobbed between the rows of vegetables. "Nana!" Madli yelled. She stumbled through the rows of green beans, dill, and potato vines.

"What, child?" The weed Nana pulled out shed dirt.

"Soviet soldiers are here. They want our radios, bicycles, and weapons. And Valter for the Soviet army." Her voice came out scratchy and low.

Nana's eyes widened. "What?" She sprung to her feet. "Peeter, run. Get Grandpa."

"Wait." Madli grabbed Peeter with both hands. "The soldiers don't know about Kalju. Tell him to hide in the forest." Her nose was inches from his. "Do you understand?" She gave him a shake.

Peeter's eyes widened into blue saucers. He nodded and tore across the field.

"Nana, they don't know about Kalju, just Valter," Madli babbled. "I lied to them. What if they find out?" Her stomach flip-flopped in fear.

Nana's hands squeezed Madli's shoulders. "Stay calm. If they ask, tell them he went back to Tallinn." She straightened her kerchief. "Let's go back to the house."

"What about Valter?" Madli asked as they walked, arms wrapped around each other. "If he doesn't go, they'll kill him."

"Stay calm," Nana said. "We must stay calm." She clasped her hands together as though in prayer.

The soldiers loaded the bicycles and radio into the truck. As Madli drew closer to the house, a burnt smell wafted toward her. She had forgotten the bread. Madli rushed inside, grabbed a towel, and pulled out a crisp loaf from the oven. "*Kurat.*" She took out the last loaf when she heard Peeter talking to the soldiers. Holding the warm pan in the dishtowel, she hurried outside.

"Grandpa's coming, but he's old and slow." Peeter stared up at them. "Why are you called the Red Army? Your uniforms are greenish."

Madli held her breath and hoped the soldier had a curious little brother at home.

"Red is the colour of the blood of the workers," Crumpled Shirt replied. "We struggle for equality, and against the bourgeoisie."

"We are all comrades," Peeter said.

Crumpled Shirt nodded. "Good boy."

Good boy. As long as he didn't believe it. Madli exhaled as the soldiers turned their attention to Grandpa, who lumbered across the yard.

"We left the hay in middle of the field," Grandpa grumbled as he folded his arms across his chest. "You want our weapons. This way."

Madli watched with the loaf pan in one hand as the soldiers stuffed the arsenal of rifles, hunting knives and shovels into the truck. From now on, they'd fight with soup spoons and sauna ladles.

After the soldiers had climbed into the truck, she walked over to the driver's side where Crumpled Shirt sat. "Perhaps you'd like another loaf of bread. You battle for the Motherland." The words choked her. She wrapped the warm loaf in the towel and thrust it into Crumpled Shirt's hands. "Please, take this. For your hard work. I'm sorry it's burnt." Perhaps they'd remember her gesture of kindness when they found out she had lied about Kalju.

Crumpled Shirt grabbed the loaf. A flicker of warmth flashed through his brown eyes.

She stepped back and the truck roared off. To conscript more innocent young Estonian men to the Soviet army. To gather wagons, weapons, bicycles, axes, shovels, tools, and anything else the Soviets wanted as they fought for their so-called equality.

Silence settled over the farmyard. The soldiers were gone and they were still alive. Madli's knees threatened to buckle.

Puzzlement registered on Grandpa's and Nana's faces.

"I offered them food so they'd like us." Madli shrugged. "Where's Valter? Does he know yet?"

Grandpa twisted away. His shoulders quivered. Nana's tears flowed down her delicate cheeks. Arm in arm they walked back into the house.

Madli took Peeter's hand. "Come on."

The flimsy white conscription notice lay in the middle of the empty kitchen table. Paper could be burned, thrown out, ignored. But not this piece. It would change lives, kill and maim with its words. The scent of fresh bread turned Madli's stomach.

"Where's Kalju?" Madli sunk into a kitchen chair, twisting the hem of her skirt.

"The forest." Grandpa pulled out the chair on the other side of the table and sat down. He buried his head in his hands.

Madli drew a deep breath. "I'll take him clothes and food

later." Practical matters were easily dealt with. The knot in her stomach was permanent.

Heavy steps pounded on the porch and Valter burst into the room. He grabbed the conscription notice. "Why me?" Valter spat. "What about Kalju?"

"They had your name." A lump in her throat choked her words.

"What if Valter doesn't want to go?" Peeter asked.

"The Soviets don't care about his feelings, only his ability to carry a weapon. They want hands to carry rifles and shoot at the Nazis." Madli told them about Stalin's speech.

"Scorched earth," Grandpa said. "Not a single pound of grain or gallon of fuel." His gaze travelled around the kitchen and he sat up straighter. His fist crashed onto the table. "They'll have to kill me before they torch this place. They won't destroy it while there's a breath in my body."

"We can always build again." Nana pressed her lips together as she fumbled for Grandpa's hand. "I wonder how many other young men have been conscripted."

A chill ran the length of Madli's spine. She'd forgotten about Toomas. She sprung to her feet. "I must warn Toomas." Her feet were ready to run in two different directions. The top of her head would shoot into space any second. Nana's words about Kalju came to mind. "If they believe Toomas is travelling, they can't conscript him."

"Why didn't you say I was travelling?" Valter asked.

Madli shook her head. "I couldn't think fast enough." She paused. "What about Kalju?"

"Kalju is safe in the woods," Nana said. "I'll take him food and clothes later. Go to Toomas."

"Kalju can't go into the army," Madli said, desperate that they understand her brother hated the sight of blood. "He hates combat. He can't bear the sight of a chicken being slaughtered."

Despite Kalju's tough opinions, he wasn't tough at all.

A feeling Madli couldn't identify crossed Valter's face. Anger? Sadness? She didn't take time to speculate. "Our bikes are gone. I'll run. It won't take me long." She hurried toward the door.

Valter followed her out of the house. "Wait."

He grabbed her shoulder. His fingers dug into her flesh.

"Ow." She twisted to loosen his grip. "I'll be back." Madli shoved him away.

Valter's lips were a thin line. "You can't risk you life. If the Soviets associate you with Toomas, they'll deport you as well."

Madli shook him off.

"If they want Toomas, you can't save him." His voice rose. "His family are rabid partisans."

Madli let the words slide out of her mind, but in one dark corner of her brain she knew he was right. Toomas and his family didn't hold back their notions about the occupation. His father actively supported a free Estonia. They'd been called dissidents and much worse.

"Stay." Valter's hazel eyes pleaded.

It was impossible to return to the house. Unthinkable to do nothing. "I won't be long."

CHAPTER FIFTEEN

Madli gulped air as she tore down the gravel road. Desperate to warn Toomas, she forced her burning legs to run faster. Faster until her feet skimmed the ground. Faster until her tears dried. Until her will couldn't compel them any further.

At the turn-off to Toomas's farm she doubled over, hands on her knees, lungs screaming for oxygen.

The ground shuddered. A truck engine rumbled from the path to the farm. Goosebumps popped on her arms.

Madli scrambled into the bushes and hurled herself to the ground. A branch scratched her left cheek, while rocks gouged her knees. "*Kurat.*" Her fingers flew to her face and came away smeared with blood. She peered through the branches. A truck, similar to the one used to deport the Kiiks, rattled around the corner and roared past. The driver wore the unmistakable cap of a Soviet soldier. In the open back of the truck stood Silvi, her parents, and a dozen other people. A blond teenage boy, his head in his hands, sat beside Silvi. Toomas.

Madli's hand shot up in a wave then quickly she jerked it down.

Her stomach heaved. The vision of the Kiiks' deportation played over in her mind. Bile rose to plant a bitter taste in her mouth.

A scream rose in her throat. It came out a whisper. "I didn't mean what I said."

Her hands gripped the earth as it spun out of control. Salt from her tears stung the scratch on her face. She relished the burn. It didn't come close to the pain in her heart. Silently the tears flowed down her face as her mind grasped for understanding. *"Mis ma teen?"* What to do? Nausea crawled through her stomach, up to her mouth. A rumble shook the road as another truck full of people rolled by. Finally she heard her thoughts, not the pounding of her heart.

Papa was gone. Toomas was gone. Their last image of her was a selfish, foolish girl, determined to get her own way. Not the caring girl who cherished their love.

An image of Mama following Papa's arrest flashed through her mind. Jaw strong, eyes glistening, hands twisting the hem of her dress. Mama's words echoed. *Papa needs us to be strong. He's smarter than a million Red Army soldiers.* Fresh tears stung. Easier said than done.

Leaves filtered the warmth of the sun on her forehead.

Finally, the sun landed squarely in her eyes. How long had she lain there? She had to return to the farm. The voice of the little girl on the train reverberated in her ears. *Do you have food?* Toomas and Silvi and their family were gone. With luck and the random compassion of a Soviet soldier, they had time to pack warm clothes and supplies for the journey.

Leaden legs took her back to the farm as one ear listened for the rumble of trucks.

Madli stumbled into the kitchen. Where was everyone? A fresh fountain of tears pushed up. She wiped them away with the hem of her skirt. Queasiness drove her to pace around the kitchen. The soldiers wouldn't have returned. Would they?

Grandpa and the boys were probably in the field harvesting hay. They'd try to get as much done as possible since they'd be one person short after tomorrow. Nana and Peeter would be weeding. Life on the farm continued.

Outside, Madli staggered toward the vegetable patch. The sight of Nana's blue kerchief in the tomato patch triggered uncontrollable sobs. She raced toward Nana and crumpled into her arms. "They've taken Toomas and his family," Madli bawled into Nana's shoulder.

"What?" Nana sputtered.

Her frail grandmother propped her up.

Madli's words spurted out, jagged and sparse, to tell Nana about the truck. "What do we do?"

Nana's eyes widened to two blue orbs. "I can't believe it."

"Why would the Soviets want to deport Toomas?" But Madli knew the answer. Valter was right: anyone with a hint of partisan allegiance would be a target for deportation.

The earthy smell of the lush vegetable garden and the heat of the sun drew fresh tears from Madli. The same summer sun would beat down on Toomas and his family and hundreds of other people as they arrived at Heltermaa Harbour. Mouths parched, stomachs rumbling and heads hurting, they'd be corralled like sheep. Madli buried her face in Nana's damp shoulder.

"Come," Nana said.

Madli let herself be guided back to the house. A warm summer day, so full of promise, held nothing but fear and anger.

Nana went straight to the pantry and returned with a bottle of vodka. She slammed two shot glasses on the table and filled them to the top. "Here. Drink." She drained hers. "Now."

Madli had never drunk a full shot of vodka. She grabbed the glass. The alcohol burned her lips and scorched all the way to her stomach where it fuelled anger and fear. To stay would be tempting fate. The Soviets had deported hundreds of families from the mainland and they still gathered people. No one was safe.

"We must hide," Madli said, her voice surprisingly strong. "The woods are the safest place." The vodka focused her. "Peeter, go upstairs and pack your things."

"Where are we going?" he asked in a small voice.

"The woods," Madli said. With mosquitoes, spiders, snakes, and ants. And safety. "Go quick."

As Peeter left, Madli realized she hadn't asked Nana. "Nana?"

Nana's expression reminded Madli of a baby deer. As if the slightest movement would startle her and she'd run.

"We must go," Madli said in a quiet voice. "Staying here is crazy." Nana would never let her go alone. She braced herself to defend her decision.

Tears crystallized Nana's blue eyes. "You should go." She waved her hand. "Go pack."

Madli opened her mouth, then closed it.

In her room, she stuffed all her clothes into the suitcase, along with her winter coat, diary, and Liisu, her doll. Linens and blankets went into a bag. As she touched the dried flowers Toomas had given her on Midsummer night, a few blossoms crumbled and fell to the floor. Her tears dripped onto the dead blossoms. She kissed the flowers and tucked them back under her pillow. She couldn't think about Toomas. Her only goal was to keep her Peeter and Kalju safe.

Madli dragged her things to the porch.

Peeter sat silent on the steps with Pontu's head resting in his lap. Nana sat on his other side, hands clasped.

Madli paced up and down the porch, set to dash into the woods at the faintest crunch of gravel. She hated sleeping in the woods. Every noise at night was magnified. A squirrel crashing through the trees would sound like a boar.

Gravel crunched.

Her head whipped around.

Grandpa stomped along the road with Valter behind.

"What's going on here?" Grandpa's gaze bounced from the suitcases to Madli. Fury lines formed a trench between his eyebrows.

"We're going to hide in the forest." Madli hesitated. "Are you and Nana coming?"

A vein on Grandpa's forehead distended. "They've taken my land. They've taken my freedom. Now they've taken Valter." Grandpa thundered up the porch steps, sending Pontu scurrying. "They arrested my son. I'll be damned if they take my farm. I won't slink off into the woods like a wounded animal."

"Instead, you'll leave me penniless and a widow mourning the stupidity of her husband," Nana said quietly.

Madli attempted to persuade him. "Grandpa, please." Given the opportunity, he'd single-handedly wrestle the Soviet army.

He stomped into the house. Nana rose, shook her head and followed him.

Madli hadn't considered Grandpa's losses. Papa in jail, Valter conscripted to the Soviet army, his farm a target for a Soviet-style bonfire. He was stubborn. Like Papa.

Like all of them.

"Where are you going?" Valter asked.

"The woods," she said.

"I don't want to sleep in the woods," Peeter whispered.

Madli sat down beside him. Of course he didn't. Neither did she. Where else could they go? If they stayed on the farm, she'd bite her fingernails to the quick. If anything happened to the boys, she'd never forgive herself.

Another option emerged. After the Kiiks had been arrested, they'd hidden in their apartment. "Maybe there is a better place," Madli said. "Toomas's farm." His name strangled her. "They won't search there, at least today."

"I'll help you carry your things over." Valter squeezed her shoulders.

The gesture melted her and for a moment her head leaned against his broad chest. She imagined his lips brushed her hair.

Madli found Nana peeling potatoes at the kitchen table. She watched the graceful movement of the knife as it created a paper-thin peel. "Nana, we're going to hide in the old threshing barn on Toomas's farm." She had no idea what remained of the building after years of disuse, but at least they'd be sheltered from bugs and animals.

Nana's lips pursed. "Good idea." Her knife continued its journey around the potato. "I'll tell Kalju to meet you there."

Nana's kerchief was slightly crooked. Madli tugged it straight. "I'll come back tomorrow for more food."

"Be careful." Nana's eyes reflected her emotions. *Be careful, stay out of sight, I love you.*

Madli hurried along the road with Peeter and Valter, her ears straining for the telltale rumble of Soviet trucks. At the corner they ducked into the forest and picked their way along a buried path to the old threshing barn. The cool of the forest soothed her hot nerves the way a cold cloth took the edge off a fever. Cool, clear thinking would keep them a step ahead of the

Soviets. Panic could cause mistakes. Mistakes could get them killed.

The wide silvery grey roof of the threshing barn blended with the surrounding field and forest which had grown in around it. Decades ago it was the main building of the farm, used for threshing and winnowing grain as well as keeping oxen and horses over the winter. In long-past summers, it made a good dance floor and master bedroom. Small doors, tiny windows and a thick thatch roof made it resemble a cottage in a medieval fairy tale.

Madli pushed open the solid wood door and ducked inside.

"Mind the high threshold," she cautioned the boys.

Her eyes adjusted to the dim light. The smell of bitter smoke from countless fires lingered. The massive oven dominated one corner of the room. It was almost as tall as Madli, and larger than her tiny summer bedroom, she was sure. There was an identical one in Grandpa's threshing barn, and Papa had told her he used to sleep on the top of the oven on frosty winter nights. Most of the furniture inside the barn had been removed. A long table remained, along with a couple of very short beds. Dirty windows over the table filtered in grey light. She set her suitcase on the limestone floor.

Valter tossed the other bag onto the bed and sat down at the table.

"I'm chilled." Peeter flopped onto the bed in the corner and shivered.

Madli pulled a blanket from her bag and tucked it in around him. "Useful for mosquito protection as well." Candlelight would be nice. Tomorrow, she'd fetch blackout fabric for the windows. "I wish Grandpa and Nana had come with us." Her voice was calm, but anger stirred in the pit of her stomach. Their stubbornness was no match for the tentacles of the Soviet army.

A knock on the door echoed in the nearly empty room. Madli jumped and landed with her fists clenched.

The door opened, and Kalju peered inside. "At least I won't be eaten alive by mosquitoes." He came in and tossed a bag on the floor. "Hey, Peeter. Move over." He threw himself beside Peeter on the narrow bed. Kalju looked as though he had aged five years. The line of his chin was sharper and the set of his mouth firm. Any boyish traces had vanished.

Madli sat down at the table and rested her chin in her hands. "They took Toomas and his family." The words, thick and heavy, hung in the air.

"I know." Kalju ran a hand through his hair and examined his nails. A long silence passed. "It's a matter of time before they find me as well." He fished through his bag and pulled out a thick branch and a knife.

"Don't say that." Madli waved her hands nervously. "You'll hide in the woods. I'll bring you food for as long as necessary. Even if it's years and years, and then my children will bring you food." She was only half kidding.

Kalju whittled the piece of wood. A smile tugged at his lips.

"Are you going to fight?" Peeter asked.

"Makes me want to." A chip of wood flew from the branch.

"You can't slaughter a chicken," Madli said. "You wouldn't last a moment in the Soviet army."

"If the Nazis get close enough, I may join them," Kalju said.

Madli's hands froze. "No."

"If that's what it takes to stop the Soviets." The knife scooped out more wood. "The Nazis are the lesser of two evils."

"How can you say that? You know they hate the Jews. Plus, Mama would ..." Madli couldn't finish the sentence. "If anything happens to you ..."

"You'd tell her ..." Kalju paused. "And Papa, that I made a

decision for my country. Papa would understand that." Wood chips dropped as he gouged the branch.

It was a lie. "Papa hates war." Madli's voice rose. "He believes in diplomacy, words, negotiation — not killing." Violence was completely out of character for Kalju. He'd see the whites of the enemies' eyes, ponder about their family, hesitate to pull the trigger, and would get killed on the first day. "You hate the sight of blood."

"I can't hide in the barn and wait for the war to end," Kalju said. "It's not right."

"You can't throw yourself into the line of fire either," Madli shouted. "What good is that?" Fear gripped her heart. He had that implacable expression she'd encountered twice. The first time was when he'd told Papa he wanted to study physics instead of history. The second was when Papa had been arrested.

Valter snorted. "With the Nazis? At least I'll be fighting against those toads."

"Why is it better to fight for the Soviets?" Madli asked in horror.

"The Nazis believe in *kinder, kirche, und kuchen.*" Valter spat out the last three words.

Kalju's knife hung in mid-air. "Children, church, and cooking," he repeated.

"At least Communism promotes equality," Valter said. "For Nazis, women are meant for breeding children and raising families." He straightened up. "I can fight for equality. I can't fight for oppression."

"We've hated the German barons who ruled Estonia for hundreds of years," Madli said. "Yet in one year, the Soviets have done such horrible things we're considering welcoming the Germans back. The Soviets kill and deport innocent people. What would you call that? I'd call it oppression."

"What about you?" Valter spun to face Madli. "If you could, who would you fight for?"

"Girls don't fight," Peeter said. "Who'd cook our meals and wash our clothes?"

Her mouth opened to retort that she would hoist a rifle if she had to.

"We're pawns," Kalju said. "At least you're fighting for your people."

Valter stiffened. "My people?"

"You're Russian," Kalju said, knife poised.

Valter's jaw stiffened and his fists balled. "Yeah. My father was Russian."

The tension in the air was similar to a thunderstorm before lighting struck. The hair on Madli's arms rose.

The accusation, thick with malice, echoed. Valter didn't move.

"You imagine I want to kill Estonians because Russian blood flows through my veins." Valter's voice dripped ice.

"There are worse excuses," Kalju said. "There are brothers battling against brothers in this crazy war. So-called friends betraying their oldest pals." His knife dug into the branch. "It's happened every day since the Red Army marched in. A person gets a whiff of power, then he wants a taste, and soon he wants an entire meal plus dessert." The knife twisted deep into the branch. "So why not?"

Valter stood up. He hadn't blinked. "I'm going."

Kalju avoided Valter's eyes. "Be careful. Try not to shoot any Estonians. Aim high."

Valter's jaw dropped. "Madli, come outside for a minute." His voice cracked. Back stiff, he strode out the door.

The temperature dropped inside the barn. The words rang in her ears.

Madli shot a scathing glance at Kalju. "You may never see him again. Apologize."

Kalju ignored her command. The knife swirled into the wood. The shape of a bird emerged.

Madli knew Kalju's moods. He wouldn't apologize.

"Kalju," Madli pleaded. "You should apologize." Her throat tightened. "I said things to Papa and Toomas the last time I saw them. I wish I could take all those words back. Don't do the same."

Implacable, he whittled the beak to a sharp point.

"What has gotten into you?"

The shock of Valter's conscription, Toomas's arrest. The pain of Papa's detention.

As Madli left, she pulled the door shut.

Valter sat rigid on the old wooden bench along the wall. He glowed with anger.

Madli sat gingerly beside him as if sudden movement would be the catalyst for an explosion.

"What the hell was that?" Valter asked, his face crimson.

Madli shrugged. "He's scared. We all are."

The forest had grown in close to the barn. Handy if they needed to bolt from soldiers. The old timber fence was buried under long grass and small trees. A clump of daisies struggled toward the light in the corner of the yard.

"I can't refuse a personal invitation from the Soviet army," Valter said.

A reluctant smile crossed Madli's face. "They'd find you, wouldn't they?" She pulled on a thread in the hem of her skirt. Find him, kill him and his family. Burn the farm.

"I need to pack." His voice broke at the end of the sentence.

Saying goodbye was unimaginable. "You'll be back. The war will be over soon." The words rang hollow, but there was nothing else to say. If she let her emotions out, she'd run screaming into the woods.

Valter wrapped his arms around her.

For a second, she pretended he was Toomas.

"I wish things were different," Valter murmured.

Thursday, July 3, 1941

Kallis Papa,

"No people, no problem." No Papa, no Toomas, and soon no Valter. And possibly no country. What would happen if there was no one left to fight? The Soviets continue to deport Estonians. They're shooting bandits and deserters on sight. The family members of these people are also targets for arrest and torture. Our lives are worthless.

To think we may have to support the Nazis. The Soviets want to burn our homes to the ground and kill everyone. Hard to believe I'm hoping for the Nazis to arrive. They're expected to enter southern Estonia within days.

I hate them all.

In the morning Madli woke up and looked for Peeter and Kalju. Kalju snored gently on the bed. Peeter was nowhere in sight.

She leapt out of bed. "Peeter." A quick scan of the room showed no sign of him. She rushed to open the front door. The morning sun exploded into her face, blinding her. She shielded her eyes.

Peeter sat in the sun against the wall of the barn. He peered into his old wooden kaleidoscope. "The sun makes the colours so bright."

Relieved, Madli sunk down beside him and reached for the toy. She twirled it and peered inside. "I love the different patterns and colours." Colours through a prism. "And the way they keep changing." Royal purple, flaming orange, midsummer sky blue, and molten yellow dazzled her eyes.

Maybe it was the childhood memory of playing with the kaleidoscope Papa had given her, or maybe it was the sky blue — Papa's favourite colour — but something made her think of him, and of the part of him she was protecting.

The manuscript.

It was still under the mattress in the summer bedroom.

Her palms began to sweat and she wiped them on her skirt. The Soviets could burn the house or destroy the farm. Scorched earth.

When Madli had taken Papa's manuscript on that cold night in November, she was confident she would mail it out of the country or smuggle it to another professor. Foolish, naïve ideas. Despite her father's status, no one would risk their life for pieces of paper. Except for her. One day, his words would matter. The truth would matter.

"Peeter, I'm going to the farm," Madli said. "You stay with Kalju. Inside." She pulled him to his feet and led him into the house.

"Bolt the door."

CHAPTER SIXTEEN

Each step back to the farm seemed a mile.

Madli's fear almost got the better of her, as she imagined Soviet soldiers bursting into the house, bayonets pointed. Grandpa and Nana escorted to the truck. They'd torch the house. Charred remains would be smouldering when she arrived.

She ran.

A glimmer of yellow appeared through the trees. She ran faster. More yellow — but it was the flash of windows in the sunlight.

A lump swelled in her throat. Thank goodness.

Madli bounded up the steps to her bedroom and opened the door. All was the same. She fell to the floor and ran her hand between the mattress and the wood bedframe. Where was it? Her elbow disappeared under the mattress.

Finally, her fingers brushed paper. Her hand still under the mattress, Madli sat on the floor. Touching the paper reminded her of Papa, sitting in his study late at night with a dim light. The smoke from his cigar. As a little girl, she'd sneak downstairs to visit him before Mama shooed her upstairs.

Freedom wasn't a dream. It had actually happened.

Madli pulled out the bundle of papers and cradled it in her lap. The true history of Estonia. The forced Soviet occupation. Last year's staged elections that voted in a puppet government. The Molotov-Ribbentrop Pact. The secret agreement that divided northern and eastern Europe into spheres of influence. Finland, Estonia, and Latvia were assigned to the Soviet sphere of influence, while Poland and Lithuania went to the Nazis. Pawns in a massive chess game. The world had to know about the injustice.

Her rage simmered.

"What are you doing?"

Madli draped her skirt over the papers. "Valter." Her stomach cramped.

"The door was open." He picked up the cover page. "What's this?"

"Only papers." She grabbed at it, but he held it high as he read the title.

"*Eesti Ajalugu.*" His brows drew together. "By Jaak Sepp. Your father." His eyes flew open. "He wrote this history book. What are you doing with it?"

Madli snatched the paper out of his hands. "It's mine." She felt as though Valter had caught her in her underwear. She tucked the papers into their envelope and hugged it tight. "Don't tell anyone. I'm keeping it safe for Papa. It's his most recent work." She didn't explain that it was a document which put all their lives in danger.

Valter's eyes remained wide. "Burn it before you get arrested." He held out his hand. "Give it to me. I'll destroy it."

"No." Madli shook her head. "One day the world will learn the truth."

"His version of the truth." Valter edged closer. "It's not worth the risk."

Killed. For words on paper. Two years ago, the concept alone would've been unbelievable.

"How did you get it?" Valter leaned back. "Didn't they destroy his papers?"

"I saw them arrest Papa that night in November. I arrived as the police escorted him out of the building." Madli stared at the embroidered flowers on bedspread till the colours blurred. "Afterward, I waited. I couldn't move for ages. It was so cold and I was so scared." She shivered. "When everyone had left, I went to his office." Her throat thickened. "I had to save the manuscript." The dark hallway had been eerily quiet as her boots squelched on the wood floor. She'd never broken any rules. Of course, there was a time when rules made sense. "The lights were still on in his office and the papers were on the corner of his desk." Her voice hardened. "One day, the world will listen to his words. The British, the Americans, they must understand our situation." The papers were almost as precious as Papa.

Valter shook his head, in disbelief or perhaps respect. She couldn't tell. His eyes were unreadable.

His lips compressed. "Are you crazy? Burn it. Rip it up."

"No," Madli spat out. She tucked the papers underneath her the way a child would hide a toy from a sibling.

"What could you possibly do with it? Other than be branded a traitor."

The answer was nothing, though over the past months she'd crafted a different story. One with a happy ending. One in which Papa's work would be published and the truth would be told. His pride in her would glow like a bright light. She couldn't let go of that dream, a speck of hope in a crazy world.

Valter shook his head, clearly frustrated. He ran his hand through his hair. "I'm leaving." Chocolate eyes bored into hers.

Sadness pierced her. "I'm sorry." The notion of never seeing him again was absurd. She sat motionless.

"I don't want to go." His shoulders sagged. "Just to get shot by a baby-faced Nazi."

"If you see Toomas, tell him ..."

Valter's eyes narrowed.

She wanted to pull back her words. "Never mind." Heat crept into her cheeks.

Annoyance flashed over Valter's face. His eyebrows pulled together.

"Grandpa and Nana need you to come back," Madli said.

Valter's frown deepened. "And you?"

"Of course I want you to be safe."

Valter leaned closer until she could smell nervous sweat. "With any luck this war will be over quickly."

His warm hands clasped hers.

Outside, Grandpa yelled, "Valter, we're leaving."

Madli raised her gaze and wasn't surprised to find his face inches from hers, his eyes focused on her lips. Their lips met in a firm kiss that lasted longer than she expected. Her eyes closed. She was tempted to wrap her hands around his neck. Only because he was leaving, she told herself. And she was scared. She released herself from the kiss. "Be careful, Valter."

A final touch to her hair, an enigmatic glance, and he was gone.

Her fingers stroked her lips. Hardly a cousinly kiss.

Grandpa's voice hailed Valter again. His footsteps pounded down the steps and she heard the commotion as bags were tossed in the back of the wagon. The clop of hooves faded.

Madli wrapped up the manuscript in an old pillowcase, tucked it into her bag, and went to the main house.

Nana bustled around the kitchen, cleaning everything in sight. She'd taken all the dishes out of the cupboard and was standing on a chair scrubbing the shelves so thoroughly that Madli wondered if any paint would remain.

"Nana," Madli said gently. "Shall I stay with you until Grandpa returns?"

Nana's red-rimmed eyes were filled with anguish. "No. Go back to Kalju and Peeter." She scrubbed the corner of the cabinet. "I put aside lots of food for you. It's in the bag in the pantry."

"I'll come back soon," Madli said. Finding words was impossible; she left, thankful to head into the safety of the forest. She had to believe that Valter would be fine. He was strong and young and capable. The war would be over before long.

Back at the threshing barn, the boys were outside picking berries. Madli stashed the manuscript inside the the massive oven; if the barn burned the oven would remain intact. "Don't worry, I won't forget this time," she said, feeling slightly foolish talking to a pile of paper.

⬚

Early Sunday morning Madli zigzagged through the forest, swatting furiously at the mosquitoes. She leapt over a fallen log and sprinted to her grandparents' farmhouse, already tasting the fresh bread and milk. She hadn't seen her grandparents since Valter left, and had to find out what had happened at the harbour on Friday. She burst into the kitchen.

"Rain is coming," Madli gasped. "The mosquitoes are vicious this morning." Silence halted her in her tracks.

Nana and Grandpa sat across from each other, both staring

into their half-eaten porridge bowls. "I dreamt of the Midnight Mother spinning." Nana twisted her spoon in her porridge.

For generations, Estonians had believed that string left on a spinning wheel overnight would be spun by the *ööema*, the Midnight Mother: a restless ghost whose spinning would be heard throughout the house, but who could not be seen at her work. The sound of the wheel being spun by the Midnight Mother was an ill omen, signifying that someone was going to die.

Madli shuddered. An old superstition, but one that now seemed ominously true. She didn't want to believe it. "Maybe the storks were clacking their beaks," she said.

Nana shook her head.

"Many people will die as the Nazis battle their way through Estonia," Grandpa said. "You're not very clairvoyant."

Nana shot him a glare. "This ghost was very restless. I heard the spinning wheel whirring and knocking." She smoothed a few grey wisps of hair into her dishevelled bun.

"Did you see Toomas at the harbour?" Hope and fear tangled in Madli's stomach.

Grandpa rubbed his temples, as if to erase the vision. "Countless men and boys were waiting at Heltermaa. Plus dozens of families were taken yesterday. Kukk, Meri, Kõiv, Kotkas."

Would there be anybody left? Madli's despair was a dark, deep hole.

"There's food for our friends hiding in the forest," Grandpa said. "Can you take it to them?" On either side of his mouth vertical trenches emphasized his anxiety.

Mosquitoes would eat her alive, but what else was there to do? She had nothing but time. She packed up the supplies and made her way through the forest, swiping away mosquitoes with an especially large branch. Despite the buzzing of ravenous insects, the cool darkness of the forest worked its serene magic to instil a sense of calm. Toomas said battles were successfully fought in the forest, not the field.

As she neared the camp, the same man from the previous day challenged her. After recognizing her, though, he greeted her like an old friend. "I'll always recognize you with those beautiful eyes." He waved her on.

Thank goodness for two differently coloured eyes.

At camp, the atmosphere hummed with energy. Conversation was louder, almost boisterous. The men strode with more confidence. Jaan waved to Madli as he stood with a group of men. "Have you heard?" Jaan punched his fist in the air. "The Forest Brothers took Kilingi-Nõmme a couple of days ago. We're helping the Nazis advance through southwest Estonia. It's fantastic."

A surge of optimism coursed through Madli. The Soviets were actually being defeated by the Estonians. Impossible but true. "What happened?"

"The Soviets were going to execute people and bury them in a mass grave, but we ambushed them at Liivimägi." Jaan's face held a broad grin. "He who digs a pit for another will fall into it himself."

She ran back to the farm so fast the mosquitoes couldn't catch her.

"I knew it," Grandpa said. "We'll be flying the blue, black, and white flag soon."

As she walked back to the threshing barn, guilt nagged at her. Cheering for the Nazis. What a warped world. The old rules of right and wrong twisted together in kaleidoscope hues of Soviet grey, Nazi khaki, and flashes of blue, black, and white.

⬚

Madli prepared a simple evening meal for Peeter and Kalju. Fear hadn't dampened their appetites, though her stomach remained knotted. As they ate, Madli told them about the Forest Brothers.

"It shouldn't take long for the Nazis to conquer Hiiumaa," Madli said. "We only need to stay hidden."

Wheels crunched the gravel in the yard. A car door slammed. The most terrifying sounds in the world.

CHAPTER SEVENTEEN

Madli's heart burst into a gallop. It pulled the blood from her legs, left them weak and useless.

"Oh ..." Fear sucked the words from her throat. Who knew they were here?

Kalju's eyes met hers. A jolt of electricity snapped across the air.

"Kalju, go. Run for the forest."

"Damn!" Kalju exploded off the bench. "They'll shoot me." His voice fractured.

Kurat. He was right. If he bolted out into the forest, they'd hear him and shoot him. He had to hide. But where?

Heart thumping, mouth parched, Madli scanned the room.

Under the flimsy wooden bed. Useless.

Beneath the table. Ridiculous.

Inside the old cupboard. Far too small.

Nothing.

Her hands clasped together. She pulled them toward her mouth, chewed on her index finger. Hopeless.

Her eyes landed on the massive clay oven that filled a quarter of the room. The inside was large enough to fit a person.

Yes, thank God.

Panic made her legs thick and stupid. Madli stumbled over to the oven and pried the door open. "In here. Quick."

Kalju dived into the oven. She shoved his feet in and shut the door, leaving a small crack for air. She whirled around.

Peeter sat frozen with his glass halfway to his lips. She grabbed the glass and threw it down. It shattered on the stone floor.

"Pretend you broke the glass," Madli whispered. "Cry."

His face crumpled.

"Not yet." Her hands fluttered like the wings of a helpless bird.

Trapped.

The pounding on the door pulverized any remaining shred of Madli's bravado. If she could have crawled into the oven and disappeared up the chimney like a puff of smoke, she would have.

"Open the door," a man commanded.

Madli's feet refused. She clutched the table and took one long deep breath. Not her last, she prayed.

He pounded on the wood. "Open the door."

Courage. She searched for a few shreds of courage. All the fine education she'd acquired in school was useless. Cunning and ingenuity. Those traits might save their lives.

"Now!" The door shook with the force of his thumps.

Jelly legs carried her to the entrance. It could be the last door she ever opened.

Trembling hands lifted the latch.

Madli tugged the solid wood door towards her.

Crumpled Shirt and Sweaty Collar loomed in the doorway, rifles dangling over their shoulders. Her gaze darted from one to the other. Dishevelled hair, harsh eyes, and thin lips; Crumpled Shirt's expression made her seize the edge of the door.

"Hello," came out as though she had a mouth full of sand.

Sweaty Collar looked over her shoulder to peer into the room. Hunter's eyes.

Madli sipped air, afraid to breathe. The air hung heavy, a calm before a storm.

A movement in the Jeep drew her eyes away from the soldiers. Another man sat in the shadows on the passenger side. A tiny glow appeared and disappeared. Smoker puffed a cigarette.

"Where's Kalju?" Crumpled Shirt stared with lizard-like coolness.

How could they know? Madli was a fly, seconds from being devoured.

"Would you like milk or water? I have fresh bread." She uttered two sentences and didn't collapse from fear.

Crumpled Shirt leaned his greasy face toward her. "Did you believe you could hide him?"

Madli drew her head back.

"You lied to us." Crumpled Shirt hurled the words toward her.

Spittle scalded her cheeks. Madli's stomach lurched. She forced herself to hold his gaze. Brown eyes with no hint of compassion destroyed any hope. She wiped her cheek on the top of her arm. Twice.

"It is by the order of Stalin that all able-bodied men must join the Soviet army. Where is he?" Yellow teeth bared.

"I ... He's back in Tallinn," Madli stuttered. "He left days ago." Her legs threatened to fold. She tightened her grip on the door.

"Liar!" He straightened up, squared his shoulders. "We heard the noise before you answered the door. Where is he?"

"The noise?" Madli widened her eyes. "Peeter dropped his glass on the floor." Madli drew the deepest breath she could. She had to convince them Kalju was gone. If her heart didn't pound out of her chest and land on the floor.

"Kalju is here," Sweaty Collar stated. "We'll wait 'til he comes back."

With a quick hand on her shoulder, he thrust her aside. Madli clung to the door and skidded into the wall. The impact rattled her teeth, rattled her nerves. Inside the house, the soldiers might notice the oven and how big it was. That it could hold a person. Her knees trembled.

Cunning and ingenuity. Madli couldn't lie with conviction.

Crumpled Shirt followed Sweaty Collar. They propped their rifles against the wall behind the table. Crumpled Shirt stood beside the oven door.

Madli arranged her face into a mask. She tried to narrow her eyes to their normal size.

Sweaty Collar swung a leg over the bench beside Peeter, who immediately scooted to the far end of the bench. "We'll take him." He gestured to Peeter. "When he grows up he'll be a traitor." He picked at something between his teeth.

The bastards. "He's a boy." Madli flung herself beside Peeter and threw her arms around him. The trembling of his thin body infused her with strength. "I told you Kalju is not here, so it'll be a long wait." She tightened her grip. Defiance was her best weapon.

In a different time, these soldiers could have been attractive young men, married with pretty wives and cute children. Instead, they prowled for innocent young men. She shouldn't have wasted another loaf of bread that day.

How long could they wait?

How long could she last?

A minute crawled by.

She'd gone to the zoo in Paris with Papa. A lion had paced in its cage, restless and ravenous. That lion wanted to kill another animal. It was instinct. It was inevitable. The soldiers had the same restless energy.

She wanted to crawl out of her skin. The tension felt like the worst summer storm, hanging in the air, waiting for the first clap of thunder, the first bolt of lightning.

Sweaty Collar coughed.

Madli tightened her grip on Peeter.

Another minute slipped away.

Peeter squirmed. Patience. Calm. Eventually the soldiers would realize Kalju wasn't there and would leave.

There was no other plan.

She hummed a Soviet marching tune. To convince the soldiers she was on their side. To drown out any noises Kalju might make, like a cough or a sneeze. Peeter's soft voice cracked as he joined in.

The third soldier, Smoker, darkened the open doorway. With the light behind him, his face remained murky. Her heart hammered. At least Crumpled Shirt and Sweaty Collar were familiar in a strange way.

"Where is he?" Smoker asked.

As she heard the voice, she relaxed her hold on Peeter. "Valter?" Hope flooded her.

He didn't answer.

"Is that you?" She squinted into the shadows, hoping for salvation.

Valter stepped into the room.

He wore a new khaki shirt and leather boots. The white

armband had the red cross of the *Havitusbataljon*. This so-called People's Defence Unit was nothing but an initiative to kill innocent Estonians under Stalin's orders. Thieves, thugs, and low-lifes, Nana called them. Estonians and Russians with revenge in their hearts — determined to settle personal scores, not fight Stalin's battle. Why was he dressed like that? Madli's heart catapulted against her chest.

"Why are you here? You left a couple days ago." Madli's arms crushed Peeter. It didn't make sense. Valter had been conscripted. He was supposed to be on the mainland serving in the Red Army. She glanced around. Crumpled Shirt and Sweaty Collar didn't appear surprised to see him.

"Valter?" Madli whispered. His new uniform screamed traitor. Blood pulsed though her head, hot and loud.

"Where's Kalju?" Valter directed his question at Crumpled Shirt.

"Kalju returned to Tallinn days ago." Madli's voice sounded distant.

Valter didn't meet her eyes.

She let go of Peeter.

The same recklessness that compelled her to retrieve her father's manuscript now infused her with the nerve to confront Valter. With a few quick strides she planted herself inches from him. His face had angles and edges she'd never seen before. His gaze focused over her right shoulder. Rage churned in her stomach.

"What are you doing, Valter?" Madli demanded. She wanted to grab his hair. "Look at me." With both hands, she shoved him on the chest. The new khaki fabric slipped under her fingers.

Valter toppled backward but regained his balance. A deep flush began on his chest, spread up his neck. "I had no choice."

His eyes scanned the ceiling. "It was Siberia or this." He gestured to the band on his shirt. The People's Defence Unit.

"You had a choice?" Madli couldn't understand. The room tilted.

Pink suffused his ears. "They offered us an option. We could stay on the island and join the *Havitusbataljon* or we could join the Red Army." He continued in a flat voice as he gazed over her shoulder. "I didn't want to die." He shrugged his shoulders as if it had been a simple choice.

Havitusbataljon or Siberia. So simple. Like vanilla or chocolate.

Icy anger swept away her confusion. "Better Siberia than a traitor. How could you? You're an Estonian. Grandpa raised you like a son. You should know better!" Madli shoved him hard. "You won't even look at me." Could this be the same boy who kissed her a couple of days ago?

Long-lashed hazel eyes finally met hers. Indifferent eyes with a glimmer of light.

"I'm not his son. I'm the son of a Russian." His shoulders lifted in a tiny shrug. "I honour my family."

Run. She'd be shot. Kalju would be spared.

Run. She'd be shot and Peeter would be shot.

Run. Don't run. Run.

Valter grabbed her by the elbows. "In the Soviet Union, you're an equal. A woman can do anything in Russia. Be a doctor, lawyer, soldier. The possibilities are endless." He squeezed tighter. "What can you be here? A wife."

He was insane. To think she'd kissed him.

She flung off his grasp and stepped back. "Your moral duty is different from that of a Soviet. How can you betray Grandpa this way?"

Valter's eyes flickered. Not remorse, not conviction.

Then she understood.

Cowardice. That's what it was. Utter spinelessness. It showed in the angle of his head, the stooped shoulders, his inability to meet her eyes.

"You really are a coward." Her words slid out slow and quiet.

"I am not a coward," Valter said quietly. "The Nazis are barbarians who believe in *kinder, kirche, und kuchen*." He delivered the words with contempt.

"We have a quota to fill." Crumpled Shirt stretched his legs.

"So now we're quota?" Madli spat. "Like sheep to be corralled or eggs to be gathered?" A surge of anger threatened to wipe out whatever shreds of judgment she had left.

"You're lucky the lot of you aren't being deported. With your father in jail, you're a target. And with that manuscript ..." Valter shook his head. "If you tell me where Toomas is, maybe we can spare Kalju." His eyebrow lifted, as if he dared her to believe him.

Valter used to pull the wings off flies with the same expression. An urge to kick him between the legs made her foot jerk. Her hands balled into fists. If only she dared.

"Toomas was deported with his family," Madli said between clenched teeth. "I told you that. What kind of game are you playing?"

"I didn't see him at Heltermaa Harbour," Valter said. "Are you hiding him as well?"

Hope flashed then fizzled. Grandpa had said there were hundreds of people there.

"Where's Kalju?" Valter asked.

Bold defiance. Bolder lies. She could do it. She had to.

"Kalju is long gone." Madli kept her mask in place. "He bolted into the forest and is miles away." Her lips flubbed the lie. She couldn't draw her next breath. Would he notice?

Valter narrowed his eyes. "Kalju is not in the forest, is he?" he whispered. "I can tell if you're lying. Where is he?"

Could he tell she was going to puke over his new boots? Her mouth opened, ready to heave. Why hadn't she learned to lie properly? Always tell the truth, her parents had told her. Another lie.

"We don't have all day. I'll make her tell us." Crumpled Shirt handed the rifle to Sweaty Collar. "Here. Hold this."

Crumpled Shirt grabbed both her arms, yanked them behind her back, and propelled her toward the bed. Her feet skidded on the floor. The burn of the pain erased her nausea.

A shove from behind. She crashed onto the bed. The wool blanket scratched her cheek, his knee heavy on her back. Hot tears brimmed. She wouldn't cry.

A belt unbuckled. A zipper slipped open.

"No," she whispered. "No."

Crumpled Shirt flipped her onto her back. His trousers slid to the ground. The army shirt barely covered the dirty grey underwear.

Her finger flew to her mouth. Biting it kept the tears where they belonged.

Would Valter actually let this happen? Madli hated herself as her eyes begged her so-called cousin for help.

"Don't hurt her," Valter said.

The lack of authority in his voice lit the fuse of her rage.

"You scum," she screamed. "*Kurati venelane.*" Madli flailed, scratched, and kicked until a smack on the side of her head stopped her. Pain ripped through her head. Warmth trickled down her nose and onto her lips. Salty fluid. Blood.

Crumpled Shirt's clammy hands pinned her to the bed.

Madli went limp.

"Don't move or I'll really hurt you." His tongue flickered over his lips. "I thought you liked me the other day."

Idiot. Never. Madli slammed her eyes shut. There were two options. Struggle and be raped. Lie still and be raped. Months of fear and loathing for the Soviets filled her with strength. Her breath steadied. She'd fight. She'd injure him. Her fists clenched and feet braced. She could bite his nose.

Madli opened her eyes and concentrated on the wall. She wouldn't resist. If rape was the worst they could do, she'd endure it. Once they'd raped her, they'd go. Once they'd left, Kalju would be safe. The faster it was over, the better.

"Peeter," she croaked, her throat thick with fear. "Your magic mittens. Cover your eyes. Cover your ears."

Crumpled Shirt wedged a knee between her legs. His face leered inches away. A lizard with grey skin, yellow teeth, and breath that stank of cabbages.

Madli hummed a song to drown out the noise in her head. *Sauna taga, tiigi ääres, mängis Mikku Manniga.* It would be over quickly. *Püüdsid väiksed konna poegi.*

"Don't!" Kalju yelled from inside the oven, his voice hollow and distant. "Don't lay a hand on her!" The oven door smacked the wall.

Madli's eyes popped open. "No!" she screamed. The rape would be over, but Kalju could be gone for the rest of his life. "Kalju, you fool." The enormity of his decision left her limp and helpless. "You should have let them rape me," she whispered to no one. Nausea roiled in her stomach.

"A fool, perhaps." Kalju's feet slid out first. He landed in a heap on the floor. "But not a coward."

Tears seared her cheeks. Oh God, oh God.

"Kalju." Valter cradled his rifle.

Crumpled Shirt's hold relaxed and he straightened up. She seized the split second, drew her knees to her chest, and kicked him like the old mule Grandpa used to own.

Crumpled Shirt thumped onto his behind, legs trussed at the ankles by his trousers. "You bitch." Hatred glinted in his eyes.

"Enough," Valter said. "We have what we want."

His pseudo-authority, an attempt at compassion, added to her fury. He was a coward hiding behind Stalin's scorched earth policy. Leave no farm unburned, no family untouched.

Madli craved a weapon. Anything. A knife, a gun, a sauna ladle. To clobber him. To gouge out his lifeless eyes. To stop him. Without taking her gaze off him, she pulled down her skirt and straightened her shirt. She wiped her face and her hand came away sticky and red. If he came closer, she'd smear the blood over his face. Her fingers curved.

Kalju walked over to the bed, sat down, and threw an arm around Madli.

She encircled his waist with both arms, felt him tremble. Stupid boy. She brushed the filth from his face but only managed to smear the soot with her tears and blood. "You should have let them. What will I tell Mama?"

"I'll be fine." Kalju's eyes spoke all the things he couldn't say. "Tell her to have faith."

"That's enough," Valter said. "We need to go." His rifle gestured toward the door.

Crumpled Shirt pulled up his pants and secured his belt, all the while ignoring her.

Madli readied herself to kick him again.

Kalju tensed.

"Kalju, I'll give you a few minutes to pack your things," Valter drawled. "Or come in your underwear."

All sensation left her while Kalju gathered his belongings. Dirt from the oven coated his white shirt and clung to his brown hair.

Kalju clicked the latch of the suitcase shut. "Peeter, be good." He hugged his brother.

Tears splashed onto her hands. Madli swallowed a sob.

Kalju turned to Madli, eyes pink.

Slowly, she got to her feet. Walked over to Kalju. Madli wanted to delay his departure even for a few seconds.

His arms were steady as they embraced her. His thudding heart told another story.

"Let's go." Valter waved toward the door.

"Wait!" Madli said. She snatched her mittens from underneath her pillow. "Here, take these. They're magic mittens." Through her tears, blue and white smeared together. She groped for Kalju's hands, thrust the mittens into his sweaty fingers.

Kalju slipped the mittens on. They barely came to his wrists. "Can't hurt to have a bit of magic." He touched the mittens to his mouth and blew her a kiss.

He didn't look back. Neither did Valter.

Boots pounded on the floor, then wilted into the grass.

Madli stared out the open door.

The Jeep doors slammed shut. The engine coughed, revved, then roared out of the yard.

Madli sank to the floor on all fours. She pressed her hands into the stone, as if to stop the earth from revolving. The tears welled inside, a sea dammed from flow by sheer will.

No people, no problem. No Papa, no Toomas. And soon Kalju would be a soldier with a sweaty collar and a crumpled shirt aiming high.

A sob escaped. She couldn't cry. She had to be strong for Peeter. She wouldn't cry. If she started, she'd never stop.

Madli's hands wrung out her skirt as if it were wet laundry. Mama did the same thing with her apron when she was nervous. Madli would need to iron the skirt and she hated ironing. She smoothed it over her knees. The deep wrinkles annoyed her.

Peeter's skinny arms enveloped her shoulders. "Kalju will come back. And so will Papa."

His soft words opened the floodgates.

She bawled. Huge, gasping sobs escaped her as tears dribbled onto the stone floor. Her body shook as her soul fell into a dark hole.

She was tired of thinking.

She was tired of feeling.

In the last year, every emotion that had a name, and some that didn't, had travelled through her.

She wanted to be numb. Unfeeling. Uncaring.

Like the cold, smooth stone she sat upon.

CHAPTER EIGHTEEN

The storm of tears passed. Her breath eased into a normal rhythm, her eyes focused, the buzzing in her head diminished.

It was still light outside. The dark was in her heart.

A sparrow flew into the room through the open door, landed on the edge of a plate, and pecked at the crumbs. Madli pulled Peeter into her lap, tucked his head under her chin, and rocked back and forth. The sparrow strutted around the edge of the plate.

She didn't get up until the sparrow flew away and her tears had dried.

Nana and Grandpa had to be told about Kalju. Did they need to know about Valter? Five small words — "Valter is with the *Havitusbataljon*" — those words would destroy their spirit. To deal with their misery was more than she could handle.

Misery or deception. Fine choices.

Mama's words about Papa came back to her. Mama said he was smarter than a million Red Army soldiers. Madli had to believe Kalju was as well. The morning after Papa was arrested, Mama made porridge as always, dressed in her favourite green dress with the white collar, and went to work, her eyes puffy.

Madli kissed Peeter's hair. "Let's go get Pontu."

Madli told Nana and Grandpa about Kalju. As she spoke, each word created an additional furrow, a deeper wrinkle, and stole light from their eyes. Inarticulate in their grief, they slumped in their chairs at the kitchen table, heads in their hands, food half-eaten, tea cold.

Madli's face swelled from so much crying. Tears had been wrung out of her and she couldn't absorb more sadness.

Valter wasn't mentioned. Madli couldn't utter the words to bring such deep misery to their lives.

Madli struggled to persuade Nana and Grandpa to hide with them in the forest. She'd never raised her voice to her grandparents, or any adult, but she stood in the middle of the kitchen and screamed at them to come to their senses. Grandpa wouldn't abandon a barn full of animals or a field full of hay.

Her voice hoarse from arguing, Madli hugged her grandparents, took Peeter by the hand, and left the farmhouse. They walked back to Toomas's farm without a word spoken.

Madli shoved open the door to the threshing barn. Inside, the silence and emptiness were so thick she could barely breathe. She couldn't spend another night there.

"Pack your things, Peeter," Madli said. "We'll sleep in the forest from now on. It's not safe here." She dragged his suitcase from under the bed.

"Do you have my magic mittens?" Peeter asked.

Madli collapsed onto the bed. Magic and goodness were a foreign language. She was tempted to unravel the mittens and dangle the yarn on tree branches for the birds. But Peeter's wide blue eyes told her he needed to believe.

"Yes." She pulled out the mittens from the suitcase. "Do you want to wear them?"

Peeter nodded and pulled on the mittens.

After their belongings were packed Peeter waited outside, throwing sticks for Pontu.

One thing remained. Papa's manuscript.

Madli fetched it from the oven and hugged it close, revelling in its warmth, in the smell of the paper. The fragrance of the best years of her life. Papa in his study late at night, happy to hoist her in his lap for a few moments before bed. She'd pretend to read, not interested in his words, only in his attention.

No more. Memories were an indulgence she couldn't afford.

She sniffed the manuscript one last time. It wasn't safe to take it with her. Nights in the forest meant wet weather. Better to keep it in a dry place than expose it to the damp. Madli swathed the manuscript in oilskin and tucked it inside the oven, snug in the velvety ashes. She latched the oven door. If the threshing barn went up in flames, the clay oven would endure. She hoped.

Madli pulled the door of the threshing barn closed with a thud.

"Where are we going?" Peeter asked calmly.

Sleeping in the woods frightened her. Blackness with only the sounds of the forest. The rustle of a thousand leaves, the footsteps of every four-legged, six-legged, and eight-legged creature on the island. Her shoulders trembled in a long shudder.

Madli racked her brain. What shelter was close? A remote building, sheltered with a door that locked. Many structures dotted the farm, most of them not used.

Madli composed her voice. "Let's spend the night in the old sauna building by the sea." If nothing else, waves lapping against the shore would soothe her frazzled nerves.

By the time they arrived at the sauna she could barely lift her feet. Exhausted, she laid out blankets and linens on the sauna benches. Peeter scrambled onto the top bench.

She lay down, her arms across her chest. The tranquil scent of cedar pulled her eyelids shut.

Madli dreamt of a kaleidoscope with vibrant garden colours. A swirl of cobalt, scarlet, lavender, and sunshine yellow. The myriad colours smashed together and spewed forth the faces of Hitler and Stalin. Thick black moustaches, eyes with the glow of evil, and chunky eyebrows contorted and twisted together until she couldn't tell who was who.

She woke up shivering as cold sweat seeped from her pores. Her damp shirt smelled of cedar. Unless Hitler granted them back their freedom, he'd be another dictator with a different moustache.

Sunday, July 6, 1941

Kallis Papa,

What makes a traitor?

Cowardice? Power? Lack of conviction? Lack of love? Or just lack of bravery?

What compels someone, raised by loving people, to turn against their own?

I'll never understand.

I couldn't tell Grandpa and Nana that Valter is a traitor. But I can tell you.

One day I'll be able to tell everyone.

CHAPTER NINETEEN

Their days fell into a routine. Each morning, Madli and Peeter would take their belongings to a different place in the forest for the day. It was unlikely that anyone would find them in the sauna, but Madli couldn't take the risk. She planned a separate escape route for herself and Peeter. Her brother wanted to come with her, but she convinced him they would be better able to elude the soldiers if they went in different directions.

Most afternoons they would stop by the farm to fetch food, supplies, and treasured hugs from Nana. Nana's eyes always begged for them to stay longer, but Madli wouldn't even stay for a cup of tea — partly because she was scared of the Red Army, partly because the farm held too many memories. It was easier to avoid thinking if she didn't remember.

Once in a while, a memory would spurt into her mind, as though pressure had built up so much it required release. Toomas's half-closed eyes and parted lips as he leaned forward to kiss her. His smoky mouth. Kalju's leap from the oven when the soldiers were about to rape her. Foolish boy. Sunday breakfasts in the summer with Papa before they headed to the beach. At those times, she wanted to curl up on the floor and wait for someone to tell her it was a nightmare. Madli shoved those thoughts back into a small dark box in the back of her mind.

On a Wednesday morning in mid-July, the pitter-patter of rain on the sauna roof woke her up. Tugging the blanket up to her chin didn't warm her. The damp had soaked into her body. If only she could light a fire, but smoke would attract soldiers the way food attracted ants.

"When can we go home?" Peeter asked in a small voice from the upper bench of the sauna.

Whenever the Nazis finished battling their way up through Estonia, and whenever the Soviets completed their scorched earth tactics. Villages had been burnt to the ground across the country. The lucky people were killed quickly. The unlucky ones fled with nothing except the clothes on their backs and fear in their hearts. The really unlucky ones were tortured and left to die.

"Soon," Madli said. "A few more days. Then we'll ..." What would they do? There was no plan. "We need to be strong." She spoke more to herself than to Peeter.

Madli sat up on the bench and tugged her fingers through her dirty, matted hair, nothing like the silky gold Toomas loved to stroke. She took a section and teased out the knots with her fingers. "My hair is a nuisance." A beacon for a Soviet soldier. If a woman was only raped, she'd be lucky.

Madli shook the images out of her head. Yesterday, Nana whispered to her about a woman found in a ditch with her breasts cut off. Raped. Tortured.

Madli had to be strong. And clever in ways she had never before imagined.

"Where are my scissors?" Madli leapt off the top bench to find her suitcase. She rummaged through her belongings. "Aha." Steel caught the dim light.

"What are you doing?" Peeter asked from his corner on the top bench.

No one cared about her hair. Toomas's hands wouldn't tug it gently as he raised her face toward his for a kiss. Soldiers wouldn't rape a boy. Madli gripped the scissors with a steady hand as she examined her reflection in the tarnished mirror. A pretty girl gazed back. The startling blue eye. The calm brown eye. A lightly tanned face. Being attractive was like having a noose around her neck. The scissors snapped shut and a chunk of hair dropped to the ground. Then another. And another. A few cuts later, the pretty girl had disappeared and in her place stood a delicate young man. In a dress.

"It's safer if I'm a boy." She ruffled her shorn locks, peered into the mirror, and nodded to herself.

"Boys don't wear dresses," Peeter said.

"When we go back tomorrow, I'll borrow some old clothes." Valter's or Kalju's things. She shuddered. She couldn't afford to be sentimental. She'd wear whichever clothes fit better.

❖

A week later, Madli picked strawberries in a small open area near the sauna. A soft breeze cooled her neck as she ate the berries. The flavour, sweet and wild, lingered on her tongue. She crammed a handful into her mouth and licked her pink-tipped fingers.

"Madli." Peeter emerged from between the trees. "Yum, straw-berries." He grabbed a fistful. Within seconds, scarlet stained his lips. Tiny rivulets of pink streamed down his chin. A messy grin showing strawberry bits and small white teeth crossed his tanned face. "There's someone at Toomas's farm."

Sensation drained from her fingers. The basket of berries tilted. "What?" came out in a coarse voice.

Peeter caught the basket with both hands.

"More soldiers?" Madli's hands wrung imaginary laundry. Another encounter with the Soviet army couldn't happen. What she wouldn't do for a solid weapon, something other than Nana's dull kitchen knife that would bruise more than slice.

"Did they notice you?" She gripped Peeter's shoulders so hard he flinched.

His lips twisted as he grabbed more berries. "It was an old lady."

Madli released her grip. "One of the neighbours, perhaps?"

"I've never seen her before," Peeter replied. "She was looking in the window of the old threshing barn." He picked out the juiciest berries with red-stained hands.

Madli couldn't imagine why an old woman would bother to find her way to the threshing barn. Maybe the woman had heard gossip. News travelled quickly in a small village. The old hag likely hoped something of value had been left behind.

Madli threw her hands up. People had lost their sense of right and wrong. "She's probably looting." Another parasite.

❖

The next day Madli and Peeter headed to Nana's for food. Pontu bounded through the forest, sniffing each new tree. A few days had passed since Madli had been to the farm. Her mouth watered at the thought of fresh bread.

As Madli approached the edge of the wood near the old threshing barn, a movement in the clearing caught her eye. She placed a hand on Peeter's chest and drew a finger across her lips as she met his eyes. "Shhh. Grab Pontu." Madli pulled Peeter down into a crouch.

An elderly woman, probably the same one Peeter had spotted, peered in the small window of the threshing barn. A nosy villager scrounging for loot. The nerve of the woman. She straightened up. Pale yellow kerchief. An old green dress with a faint pattern and a faded blue cardigan with too-short sleeves. And a rifle.

The old woman opened the door of the threshing barn and entered the building. Nothing was inside. Madli had made certain. A few minutes later, the woman came out. She fumbled in her apron pocket and pulled something out.

Madli still couldn't see the woman's face.

Her rifle leaning against her legs, the woman fumbled with whatever was in her hand, then straightened up. She lit a cigarette, tilted her head back, and blew out a ring of smoke. The profile, the angle of the fingers were oddly familiar.

Madli's heart beat wildly. "Turn around," she whispered.

"What?" Peeter asked.

With trembling hands, Madli smoothed her short hair. "I know who that is." If she was wrong, they'd be killed.

"Let Pontu go," Madli said. She rustled on the ground and found a branch. She hurled it toward the clearing. "Fetch, Pontu," she whispered.

The dog bounded out of the bushes and into the clearing to chase the stick. Madli held her breath. The woman hoisted the rifle to her shoulder and took steady aim at the dog. Madli cursed herself. It hadn't occurred to her that Pontu could be shot.

The woman lowered the rifle and held out her hand. "Pontu! Come here." Pontu sniffed delicately. The woman lifted her eyes and scanned the bushes. Blue eyes. Piercing eyes. Young eyes.

"*Issand Jumal*," Madli whispered. "It's him." His blue eyes sucked all the power from her voice. "Toomas," her voice quivered. The sight of his lean face, dark with stubble, framed by the fetching yellow kerchief, caused a giggle to bubble inside of her.

Madli crashed through the bushes. "Toomas!"

He hoisted the rifle to his shoulder and aimed straight at her.

CHAPTER TWENTY

Madli remembered too late her spiky short hair, her baggy shirt, and Kalju's old brown trousers. Her arms shot up in the air in surrender. She halted, petrified. "It's me!" Her heart pounded so hard she barely heard her own words.

Toomas's blue eyes narrowed into a squint while holding the rifle steady.

"Don't shoot." Panic caused her voice to squeak. "Look at my eyes." Eyes wide, she took a couple of steps toward him. She didn't dare blink.

"Madli?" He squinted again. A wide grin crossed his face. He laid the rifle on the ground.

Madli hurled herself into his arms. Strong arms that quivered when they wrapped around her and squeezed her tight. Her breath came in gasps that quickened into chuckles. Within seconds, she was laughing so hard she slipped out of his arms and dropped to the ground, tears streaming down her face. It was hilarious.

Toomas. Here. In a dress. Disguised as a woman.

And her. In pants. Disguised as a man.

Flat on her back, she clutched her stomach, howling with laughter. "*Issand*," she gasped. "*Jumal.*" Tears streamed over her cheeks.

Toomas dropped down beside her and propped his head on his elbow. Giggling, she caressed the stubble on his cheeks. She tugged on his too-short cardigan sleeves, high on his bronzed arms. She pulled the flowered apron tied around his waist and pushed the yellow kerchief off his head. Her fingers tangled in his hair.

Toomas took her hand after Madli had touched him for the umpteenth time. "Yes, I'm real." He planted it against his warm chest and hammering heart.

"You," Madli snorted, "look so funny." She forced herself to take a couple of deep breaths. "Why are you dressed like a grand-mother?" Her hand melted into his body.

His lips curled into a crooked grin. "All the better to avoid the Soviet soldiers, find my way through the woods and along the roads."

Madli rolled onto her side to face him. "I'm sure every grand-mother carries one of those." She gestured to the rifle on the ground. "Didn't the Soviets take all the weapons? How did you get that?"

"We Forest Brothers have our ways."

Peeter plunked himself at their feet. "I thought you were going to shoot Pontu."

"What are you doing here?" Madli drank in Toomas's chis-elled features, dirty clothes, and gaunt frame. The gap between Midsummer and today was vast, littered with memories of arrests and deportations.

"I was searching for you." Toomas pursed his lips. "Your grandmother told me what happened to Kalju." His eyes radiated sympathy. "And that you and Peeter were hiding in the forest. I didn't know where else to look so I kept coming back here."

The memory of their last meeting gave her reason to blush. "Do you forgive me?" she asked in a small voice.

"For being alive?" Toomas grinned.

"No," Madli said. "For being ... difficult." Her gaze dropped to the buttons on his cardigan. "I was afraid to like you in case you were arrested. And deported."

"Which is nearly what happened," Toomas said.

Madli noticed his massive brown leather boots under the delicate long black skirt. "I wasted those moments."

Toomas lifted an eyebrow. "Definitely. Arguing was a waste of time. We could have been doing other things."

Madli blushed.

"Was it you a couple of days ago?" Peeter asked.

Toomas nodded.

"How did you get here?" Madli asked. If he told her he'd dropped from the sky she'd believe him. "I saw you and your family in the truck with the soldiers."

"I was in the outhouse when the soldiers came. When I heard the truck and Russian voices, I bolted into the woods." He rubbed his eyes. "I pray for them every night."

It hadn't been Toomas in the truck. Toomas had been saved by an urge to go to the bathroom. A giggle gurgled in her throat. Lucky boy. Had he gone half an hour later, even fifteen minutes earlier, he'd be on a train to Siberia. She stroked his hand.

Papa and Mama had always taught her to think things through, make good decisions, be responsible. They'd never mentioned luck. The kind of luck that has nothing to do with fairness or responsibility. Bad luck breaks down the door and drags an innocent man to Siberia. Good luck makes a man go to the outhouse as the soldiers travel down a narrow gravel road.

Madli told Toomas about Valter and Kalju and the soldiers. "They were going to attack me and Kalju saved me." Her throat stung. "It was stupid of him. I would've survived." Her fury with Kalju boiled over. He should have stayed hidden, but no, Kalju had to be a hero. Heroes die. Boys hiding in outhouses survive to fight another day.

With eyes that could ignite a fire, Toomas tugged out a hunk of grass. He hurled the dirt toward the trees.

"I couldn't tell Nana or Grandpa about Valter. The pain for them would be overwhelming." A lump thickened in her throat. "Best if he never comes back." Forgive and forget had been Mama's mantra. Not this time. Not ever.

Madli's hand stroked Toomas's clenched fist, filled with soil. "It's over." As she spoke, fear threatened to squelch her happiness. She shoved it back. Reliving the horror was pointless. She wanted this happy moment. She needed it.

Toomas stared into the distance, breathing fast. His fist relaxed and his fingers grasped hers.

"Later," Madli said. "We'll talk more later." *Later*. A wonderful word.

His blue eyes bored into hers as though he sought that place in her mind where her secrets were hidden.

"Later," he repeated. His eyes brightened, then lingered on her hair. "You make a handsome boy." He fluffed her wispy locks.

"I thought it would be safer." Certainly not more attractive. Heat rose in her cheeks. The sophisticated city girl was gone, replaced by a skinny young boy in dirty clothes.

Toomas grinned. "I like you for more than your hair."

"Where have you been?" Peeter asked.

"At first, I hid in the forest," Toomas answered. "Then I stumbled upon a group of Forest Brothers. More and more men joined us, as well as several women and children. It's easy to avoid the Soviets in the woods. They don't know the land like we do. I trust the trees, the shadows, the way the sun makes its mark." His eyes gleamed as he gestured. "The Forest Brothers are making enormous advances in the south of Estonia. They helped the Nazi troops take Viljandi and Pärnu. Tartu is still under siege, but it's likely we'll defeat the Soviets there as well."

"How do you know this?" Madli asked. *Victory*. A word rarely uttered. She didn't dare let hope out of its dark corner in her mind.

"We have a radio." Toomas clasped her hands between his. "No one is safe here. Stalin's army is burning farms, leaving a bloody trail of bodies on the roads and in the middle of the fields as they withdraw. Come with me." His gaze swung back and forth between Madli and Peeter. "To the Forest Brothers' camp."

Peeter's lips twisted in puzzlement. "Can Madli come along?"

"Of course. Why not?"

"Because they're the Forest Brothers, not Forest Sisters."

Madli exchanged glances with Toomas, then burst into laughter so hard she ended up flat on her back again. Cradled in the warm grass, she felt hope peer out of its dark corner. "We can all go," she said. "Together." An invisible weight eased off her shoulders. "Peeter, let's get our things. We'll go tell Nana and Grandpa."

On the way through the woods, Toomas explained how the Forest Brothers had gathered strength in both numbers and weapons to help the Nazis advance up through Estonia. "Our enemy's enemy is our friend. We'll help the Nazis defeat the Soviets."

Fear oozed into Madli's heart. "How can we support the Nazis?" she asked. Her memory flew to Sarah's fear of persecution, of the Nazis' goal to create a master race that excluded all Jews. *Judenfrei.* "So that maybe they'll be nice to us and give us back our country?" Helping the Nazis fell into the category of foolhardy, not to mention frightening.

Toomas halted. His eyes were the colour of the sky. "We can't fight the Soviets on our own. This is our country. Our tiny war in the midst of a world battle. We need to be smart, cunning, like Clever Hans, and defend ourselves in whatever way we can." His lips formed a tight line of determination.

Madli nodded, but her fear knit a tight weave around her chest. Toomas supported the Nazis. All for good and patriotic reasons. Wasn't there another choice?

When Nana saw Madli with Toomas, she almost broke out into a polka. An ear-to-ear grin, crooked teeth and all, spread over her face. When Madli told her of their plans to join the Forest Brothers, Nana immediately started to pack up food. "Take all the bread, I'll bake more. And some sausage, and how about some cheese?" Food flew into the bag. "Peeter likes *maasikamoos.*" In no time, two sacks of food sprawled on the kitchen table. Madli added a bag of old shirts and pants to the pile.

"We'll be back soon, Nana." If she said the words, they'd be true. "We will." No other option could enter her mind. Anxiety about her grandparents' safety infused her with the courage to broach the subject one more time. "Why don't you come with us?"

Her frail Nana shook her head. "I can't leave Grandpa, and he can't leave the animals and the farm." She sighed. "It is what it is."

They trekked to the Forest Brothers' camp in silence. Madli was thankful for the quiet. The green fragrance of the trees and the dark scent of the soil usually calmed her nerves. Not this time. She tried to sort out her emotions: ecstatic that Toomas was alive, devastated by the conscription of Kalju and betrayal of Valter, relieved she didn't need to protect Peeter all by herself, exhausted by the amount of transformation in her life. Thoughts collided together in her mind, each vying for attention. She had no energy to sort through them. Remaining one tiny step ahead was enough. Survival first; thinking would come afterward.

The haphazard layout of the Forest Brothers' camp had flourished into a small village. Shelters built from branches dotted the woods around the clearing. Half a dozen structures were rough lean-tos, mostly for one or two people, with enough cover to keep the rain off. Others were in the form of massive beehives with tiny low doors. A rough count of the people put the total around thirty men plus a handful of women and children she didn't recognize. Likely from neighbouring villages.

No one recognized her as a boy. Her eyes became her passport.

Jaan broke a smile and clapped her on the back. "We're happy to see you. Where's your grandfather?"

She explained Grandpa's reluctance to abandon the farm.

A frown creased Jaan's brow. "Throughout history we have always been outnumbered, and have sought refuge and strength in the mazes of the woods and swamps where no enemy dared to go. That is what a small, clever people does. An ambush from the forest over a bold attack across a field."

Madli could do nothing but nod.

"Where are we going to sleep?" Peeter asked, wide-eyed as he gazed around.

"Over here." Toomas led Madli and Peeter toward the back of the camp.

Toomas stopped at a small lean-to built partially into the hill-side. Crude and sturdy, the foliage and branches provided shelter but not much else. "The food goes in the food locker. Things we don't need we'll tuck under a tarp."

Madli kneeled down to peer inside the lean-to. Most of the tiny floor was a bed fashioned from leaves and pine needles, with a couple of blankets thrown on top.

"This makes the sauna look luxurious," she muttered.

A sob bubbled up in her throat and her eyes stung with tears. Maybe it was happiness, maybe fear, maybe just hopelessness at the overwhelming odds against surviving until her next birth-day. October was many battles away.

"It's comfortable for one, a bit cozy for two. I'm sure we can fit three," Toomas said.

Three cats wouldn't fit in the lean-to.

Madli's shoulders quivered. She couldn't break down in front of Peeter and Toomas, not when they were finally safe.

Her emotions had no use for her logic. Sobs strangled her. Toomas's hand stroked her back. Tears poured out, streamed down her hands and soaked her shirt. Finally, when the well was dry, she glanced at Toomas and Peeter. They both seemed unsure of what to do.

"How are we going to fit in here?" she gasped. "We'll be like sardines in a tin." She'd dreamt about spending time with Toomas in the summer, but not in a lean-to in the middle of the forest while eluding Soviet soldiers. Not to mention with her little brother by her side. She blushed hot. "We'll stay in here tonight. Let's talk about other choices tomorrow."

＊

That night she lay tucked between Toomas, gently snoring, and Peeter, flipping and flopping in his sleep. Pontu lay at their feet.

She inhaled the sweet scent of the woods. Forest Brothers. And Forest Sisters. She smiled and swept a hand over Peeter's soft hair. With luck, they'd be safe here.

An owl hooted. Leaves rustled. Wild creature sounds yanked her awake. Pontu would warn them of any intruders, but the feeling a wild boar would eat her toes nagged her.

Toomas's support for the Nazis tugged her back into wakefulness. Collaboration with the enemy would be unthinkable for Papa. Then again, Papa wasn't trying to stay alive while the Soviets and Nazis played monkey-in-the-middle with Estonia. Was that a good enough reason?

Tuesday, July 22, 1941

Kallis Papa,

My thoughts are too chaotic to write down. How much things have changed! The Soviets are being trounced by the Nazis, with the Forest Brothers' support. Can you imagine? Have we simply given up on the notion of right and wrong? Or have we perhaps expanded our definition? If you believe the end justifies the means, we should aid the Nazis. If we survive, perhaps all will be forgiven and forgotten. I hope so.

"Hold it further back on the barrel." Toomas adjusted her grip. "Here."

The rifle pressed into Madli's shoulder. Would she ever be angry enough, scared enough, or brave enough to point a weapon at anyone? Kalju's words to *aim high* echoed in her ears. Not if they were Soviets. What if they were Nazis?

"For a girl who studied literature, you have a steady hand." Toomas's strong hand stabilized her shoulder.

"From holding all those heavy textbooks, I've developed good muscles." It was a long way from fiction to firearms.

"The trigger has a double pull. Take up the slack on the trigger before squeezing it." Toomas let go of her hand. "Give it a try."

Heat from his body caused Madli's concentration to waver. She pulled her focus back to the heavy rifle resting in her hands. One eye closed, she aimed at the mark on the tree. Squeezed the trigger. The blast knocked her against Toomas. Shards of bark flew. "How did I do?"

"Not bad." Toomas clapped her on the back. "Pull back the bolt to empty the chamber."

Madli did, and within a few seconds she was ready to fire again.

"If you take your time like that," Toomas said. "You'll be dead." He took the rifle from her, aimed, hit the mark, snapped the bolt, and repeated. "Like this."

"You've had more practice," Madli observed. She rested the butt on the ground. "Why am I doing this? I couldn't shoot anyone." She swatted a mosquito. Rain hovered and the insects wanted a last feast.

"Not even if they had a rifle aimed at me?" Mock disappointment pulled his mouth into a pout. An irresistible pout.

A pout warmed into a kiss. Madli met his lips as the first raindrops plunked onto her head.

Toomas pulled away as the rain increased. "The rifles need to be kept dry."

Back in the lean-to, she curled up in the warmth of his arms and listened to the soothing drum of rain on the dry ground. It was the first time they'd been alone without Peeter. She twisted to face him.

"I was afraid you wouldn't be able to protect yourself. But you took care of Kalju and Peeter in the woods by yourself, and you've outwitted the Red Army more than once." Toomas nodded. "You'll do fine." He leaned toward her, eyes half closed. . "Peeter isn't here."

A surge of pride coursed through her. Bravery and cunning weren't traits she knew she possessed. Perhaps she did. Confidence nudged out her fear.

Her arms draped around his neck. She leaned close, inhaling his scent. "Enough talking."

CHAPTER TWENTY-ONE

Saturday, July 26, 1941

Kallis Papa,

It's been four days since Peeter and I moved to the Forest Brothers' camp. Already we're into a routine. At mealtimes I help the women prepare food. One of the farmers sent us a pig he had slaughtered and salted. The pig is buried in a large tin underground. It will last for a while. Another family brought their cow, so we now have milk. Yesterday I suggested we cook snails. Everyone was horrified. The snails in Hiiumaa are the size of small apples. Ten times larger than the escargots in Paris. Remember how delicious they were? Sautéed in butter and garlic. My mouth waters when I think of them. I explained snails are considered a delicacy in France but no one believed me.

Saturday, August 2, 1941

Kallis Papa,

There is excitement about the growing strength of the Forest Brothers as they help the Nazis battle their way through Estonia. The men strategize and train for the time when the Nazis land on Hiiumaa. It is hard not to hope for our country's liberation.

Peeter and I barely fit inside the lean-to Toomas built. The last few nights were rainy and cold, so another family squeezed us into their hut. A welcome respite from the rain, but I hate being in close quarters with strangers. Once the weather cleared, we went back to the lean-to.

Don't worry about me sharing the lean-to with Toomas. You won't have to reach for your shotgun. He's a perfect gentleman. It's hardly the circumstance where romance blooms.

Peeter is happy to have friends, play ball, and run in the woods. There are a couple of boys his age. Pontu follows him around and flops down exhausted in front of the lean-to every night.

We're free inside this forest cage made of spruce, pine, and birch.

Every few days, I return to Nana's for food. She keeps a white towel hanging on the porch to indicate it's safe to return. I wonder what would happen if soldiers came and she didn't have time to remove the towel. I approach through the forest, check for Jeeps, then scoot in and out. Nana cries joyful tears when she sees me and tears of sadness when I leave.

Grandpa sends more than enough food. Other farmers share their bounty with us as well. People are generous though they've been forced to give up animals and provisions to feed the Soviet army. Grandpa must be seething. I wouldn't be surprised if he turned the animals loose into the forest rather than aid the Soviets.

One farmer was asked to bring a pig to the soldiers. Instead he brought a sheep. He was arrested and held for three days. How brave of the Red Army to arrest a man with a sheep.

Sunday, August 3, 1941

Kallis Papa,

We've won! The Battle of Tartu is over and we — the Estonians — have won. Two weeks of fighting against the Soviet army, but the Forest Brothers and the Nazis defeated the red monster. It won't be long now until we're free.

What a strange experience to win against the Soviets. As much as I'm ashamed to support the Nazis, it's hard to deny that they're helping us. If we hadn't joined forces with them, I'm convinced the Soviets would have burned all of Estonia to the ground. We've heard that many Soviet conscripts have escaped and deserted to the Nazi side. I hope Kalju is wearing a Nazi uniform. It would be so much better than being in a cattle car en route to Siberia, or on a battlefield, cold and hungry.

Grandpa and Nana are beginning to take the Soviets more seriously. While Grandpa still won't leave the farm, he'll sleep in the woods when he hears that the Soviets are close by. Nana bakes bread and makes food.

Wednesday, August 6, 1941

Kallis Papa,

Everyone has lost someone — friends, family, neighbours, or all three. The number of stories is endless. Occasionally, a person's amazing good luck warms my heart.

I heard a story about a couple of families hiding in a big haybarn. The women and children were outside cooking when three Soviet soldiers turned up. The family must have been paralyzed with fear. I know I would have been. The soldiers went inside the barn and stabbed the haystacks with their daggers. The women and children screamed and, somehow, they chased the soldiers away. It turned out that the men were hiding inside the hay.

These stories offer me hope.

Thursday, August 7, 1941

Kallis Papa,

I have muscles. Real muscles. I can hoist two full pails of water easily. Digging out wet laundry from the cauldron no longer makes me gasp and sweat. I can carry at least six logs from the woods to the fire without my muscles being sore for days.

I'm flexing my arm right now. Can you picture the bulging muscle? I'm tempted to arm-wrestle with Toomas. I can beat Peeter, but it's hardly fair competition.

Sunday, August 10, 1941

Kallis Papa,

Estonia is now part of the Nazi protectorate, Ostland.
I wouldn't welcome them with open arms, but just between
you and me, I'd be happy to see the Nazi Army.

I can't believe I just wrote that sentence, but I'm
desperate to see the Soviets gone. I can't expect the Nazis
will be better, but at this moment it seems they won't be
worse. My mind swirls.

Monday, August 11, 1941

Kallis Papa,

There are days I think we'll die in these woods and the birds
will pick our bones clean. The NKVD continues to execute
families of partisans, burn their farms, and leave their
bodies in the streets and fields as a warning.

The Nazis battle their way through Estonia. The Soviets
are desperate, scared, and angry. The destruction battalions
ravage the countryside. Stories of scorched villages, bodies
of women with their breasts cut off, dead men left in the
fields, children brutalized by the soldiers. And for what
reason? Because this is war. A war we didn't ask for or want
to participate in. A war we can't begin to win.

Friday, August 15, 1941

Kallis Papa,

I heard about a father who was set free by a Soviet. The

soldiers lined up the man's three children along the side of a barn and threatened to kill them if he didn't tell them where his older boy was. He refused, of course, and was taken away to be executed. Soldiers, refugees, and farm animals littered the road. A few kilometres from the house, one of the soldiers told the father to flee into the field. Perhaps even the Soviets get tired of killing.

Another man, before he came to join us at the Forest Brothers' camp, built a bedframe inside a haystack. He had a bed with sheets and covers and slept quite comfortably, dry in the rain, warm at night and safe from Soviet eyes.

Life is luck, timing, the unexpected humanity or undeserved cruelty of a Soviet soldier.

Friday, August 22, 1941

Kallis Papa,

The Forest Brothers wage war against the destruction battalions, the Hävituspataljonid. In the course of their scorched earth tactics, the battalions have destroyed crops and cattle, as well as all sorts of industrial equipment. Courts martial are common. Anybody caught in hiding or suspected of belonging to or aiding the Forest Brothers is sentenced to death. Farms are looted and burnt down.

The Forest Brothers, in turn, eliminate members of the destruction battalions, Soviet activists, and people suspected of assisting in deportations. These people are sentenced by vigilante courts and shot.

Both sides fight to win as well as settle their personal scores.

I wonder what's happened to Valter. Though it's unhealthy to wish him dead, I have satisfaction thinking he picked the wrong side.

Wednesday, August 27, 1941

Kallis Papa,

We've built a better shelter now that the weather is cooler. Nothing too fancy since the Nazis are on our doorstep, but something that will keep out the wind and rain. It took a few days, but with help we've built a beehive shelter. A frame of thick branches surrounded by pine, spruce foliage, and leaves. We also built three bedframes, a double bunk, and a single bed. Peeter is quite handy with a saw and lashed the frame together himself. It's positively luxurious compared to the lean-to and some of the other shelters in the camp. Now we have an actual door to shield with a tarp. I can barely stand up straight in the middle of it. Toomas hunches like Quasimodo.

I put on a cheerful face for Peeter, but I'm sick of living in a mud hut. What I wouldn't do for a bath, a little perfume, some pretty clothes, and a cup of hot chocolate. I still wear Kalju's old pants and shirts. They're practical and comfortable, but ugly.

I hate to write about my complaints, but I finally had to. I cry when the boys leave the shelter. I sob into my pillow at night.

Where are you, Papa?
Where is Kalju?
Where is Mama?

Monday, September 1, 1941

Kallis Papa,

The Nazi troops and Forest Brothers arrived in Tallinn a couple of days ago. The Nazis were welcomed in the streets with traditional gifts of salt and flowers. People were so happy to see them.

Teretulemast Tallinna!

Elagu Eesti!

The blue, black, and white flag was hoisted once again on Pikk Herman. The next day the Nazis replaced it with the Swastika flag.

They let us play the Estonian national anthem. How amazing!

We're next. I can't imagine the Nazis would be worse than the Soviets.

I feel better today. Not quite as desperate and desolate.

Friday, September 12, 1941

Kallis Papa,

Gunfire and bombs wake me up. I'm no longer scared. It means salvation is getting closer.

The other day it rained paper. The Luftwaffe planes dropped leaflets, a gentle rain of white paper that showed a map of Estonia and the extent of Nazi domination. The mainland is free of the Soviets, while the smaller islands along with Saaremaa and Hiiumaa are still waiting to be liberated.

I hear bombs and my hopes rise. Today, perhaps tomorrow, surely next week the Soviets will be forced out of Hiiumaa.

The problem is that our island has been transformed into a porcupine. Meadows, pastures, fields, and farmyards are full of pointed stakes over a metre high pounded into the earth, awaiting parachutists. The beaches are dug full of ditches, aimed to trip any planes attempting to land. How can the Nazis infiltrate the island and free us?

Saturday, September 20, 1941

Kallis Papa,

Vormsi Island was freed. It's about time. But when will the Nazis land on Hiiumaa? We hear the bombs fall on Saaremaa. The calm before the storm. I can feel the tension. We're all on edge and jumpy. Weeks of living in the forest have jangled my nerves. Toomas pretends to be calm. He's with Jaan most of the time, listening to the radio and plotting a strategy to help liberate the island.

Remember when I helped you paint the floor of our pantry? I started at the door and painted myself right into a corner. Helpless and unable to move. That's how I feel now.

Thursday, September 25, 1941

Kallis Papa,

One of Nana's friends, Mrs. Part, went to village and never came back. Grandpa went to hunt for her. She's been missing for three days. There's not much hope she's alive.

Friday, September 26, 1941

Kallis Papa,

The warm days of summer shorten into the cool days of
fall. Life continues as vegetables ripen, crops are gathered,
the rye is harvested, and preparations are made for the
long, dark winter months. I'm used to the drone of planes
overhead while I tug potatoes from the soil.

Peeter and I have been helping Grandpa harvest the
fields. Vegetables, rye, and Grandpa wait for no one.

You'd recognize me again since my hair has grown out. I
no longer look like a boy. It's nice to have longer hair again.

Monday, September 29, 1941

Kallis Papa,

Michaelmas is the official end of summer and beginning of
winter. Even the Nazis on our doorstep and the desperate
retreat of the Soviets can't stop time. Custom calls for a
big celebration, or next year the hay won't grow. In honour
of the beginning of winter, Grandpa slaughtered a sheep,
Nana baked potatoes, rutabagas, and turnips, and I made
pirukad. It was a feast to end all feasts. With a watchful
eye on the driveway we ate quickly, then scooted back into
the shelter of the forest.

Thursday, October 2, 1941

Kallis Papa,

Each day the Luftwaffe and Soviet planes whine overhead.

Today was quiet and rainy so the planes were grounded. The silence is so peaceful; like a normal day. If there is anything normal about living in the middle of a forest.

Sunday, October 5, 1941

Kallis Papa,

Every day I hear more bombs on Saaremaa. Their battle has lasted weeks. Surely the Soviets can't hold out much longer. I can barely sleep, I'm so anxious. Months of hiding in the forest, sleeping in a shelter, and cooking food over an open fire may be over. The roads are muddy and have been ploughed up by tanks. Many villages have no electricity. It's a strange feeling to look forward to the Nazis. Now I think freedom is the one thing that matters. The only way to achieve freedom is to push the Soviets out of the country.

   Fuel is precious and food is getting scarce. Thank goodness for the harvest we've hidden.

Tuesday, October 7, 1941

Kallis Papa,

Yesterday, Soviet planes landed in the northern part of the island. They brought in food and ammunition, and took away injured soldiers, women, and children — almost two hundred people. The Soviets need reinforcements for their upcoming confrontation with the Nazis.

   The battle continues.

CHAPTER TWENTY-TWO

"We're next," Madli dared to say on Friday morning. She fumbled to light the lantern inside their shelter. Her fingers were sticks of ice. "I feel it in the air." The end of Soviet rule nudged nearer. Saaremaa Island had finally been conquered by the Nazis.

Madli regretted the words immediately. She didn't want to raise Peeter's hopes. The pending Nazi invasion was all people talked about. Optimism was an unfamiliar feeling.

Peeter slid off the top bunk wrapped in his blanket. "Can we go home to Tallinn?" Some days he sounded younger than his seven years. Almost four months without seeing Mama. He didn't ask about Papa. A year without a father was forever in the life of a seven-year-old. After spending weeks in the forest, he was an expert at living in the woods, but Madli heard the loneliness in his voice and wished he could have better memories of his childhood. Fun memories.

"Soon." Madli gave her usual answer. Today she meant it.

"Tomorrow?" Peeter asked.

Madli sighed. There had been so many tomorrows. They'd been hiding in the forest since the beginning of July. Over three months. She barely remembered a time without bombs and soldiers.

Toomas moaned.

"Up, sleepyhead." Madli sat down on the rickety bedframe and gently jostled his shoulder. The heat of his skin burned through his shirt. "Toomas, how do you feel?" She rested the back of her hand against his forehead. "You're burning up."

"I'm fine," Toomas said weakly. "A bit of a fever. Nothing to worry about." In the dim light, his eyes looked glazed as he attempted to keep them open. His teeth chattered together.

Madli laid another blanket on him. "Rest in bed today. You can't be sick." Along with the other men at the camp, Toomas had prepared to aid the Nazis landing on Hiiumaa.

"I know," Toomas said. "I'll be fine. Don't fuss." He rolled over on his side. "I'll be ready soon. There are more details to go over with Jaan."

When the Nazis landed near Emmaste, Estonian guides would show them the way from the beach to the roads. The operation was well organized. The Forest Brothers knew the Soviets had informants throughout the island, and that they were prepared for battle at Emmaste. But what the Soviets didn't realize was that the Nazis had better information. The man who organized the meat supply to the Soviet bases had not only been feeding the Soviets; he'd been feeding information about the location of Soviet bunkers, fortifications, and mine-fields to the Nazis.

"Don't do anything silly." Madli finished dressing. "I'm going to Nana's to help with chores. I'll bring you back milk and onion soup." She kissed his hot forehead, then beckoned Peeter. "Come on; get Pontu."

※

In Nana's kitchen Madli peeled and chopped onions, then put them in water to boil. She sat down at the kitchen table with Nana.

"Have you been able to persuade Grandpa to hide in the woods?" Madli knew the answer. The conversation had repeated itself many times.

Nana waved her hand. "He's as thick as a table leg."

Madli leaned forward. "Come with us, Nana. Please." Both of them knew Nana wouldn't leave without Grandpa. "At least persuade Grandpa to stay in the forest the next few days. He can let the animals out of the barn early in the morning."

Nana nodded, more out of habit than conviction.

When the onions had boiled, Madli scooped them into a small pot of milk and boiled the concoction again. When it was done she poured the mixture into a bottle, wrapped it in a towel and hurried back to Toomas.

※

When Madli entered the dimly lit shelter, the pungent odour of sickly sweat greeted her. A dark shape lay curled up on the bed, covered in a blanket.

"Peeter," she said. "Light the lantern." She touched the glass. Cold. It hadn't been used all day. Worry nibbled at her.

Toomas groaned as he pushed himself up to a sitting position. His sunken eyes met hers. The shadows scooped holes in his cheeks.

Madli handed him a cup of milk and onion soup.

Trembling hands gripped the cup. He slurped. A grimace

contorted his face. "My mother used to make this."

"Drink up. It'll make you sweat out the sickness and help you sleep." Madli steadied his clammy hands and guided the cup to his mouth.

Toomas gulped it down. "Can't hurt, I suppose." The cup slipped from his hands. "I'm going to rest a moment."

Madli grabbed the cup.

Within seconds, he was asleep.

Madli pulled the covers over his shoulders and brushed a hand over his forehead. Ablaze with fever.

"What if Toomas doesn't get better?" Peeter asked.

"Don't say that," Madli snapped. No one knew the woods and paths the way Toomas did. If he didn't guide the Nazis quickly and safely from their landing point, the mission would be jeopardized. Angry Soviets resembled a nest of disturbed hornets.

Saturday morning, Toomas wasn't better. Madli's hand fumbled to locate his forehead. A groan slipped out.

Toomas burned like a bonfire at Jaanipäev.

"I must go talk to Jaan." His voice hardly penetrated the dark.

Madli lit the lantern. "You're still sick." He'd end up with pneumonia if he persisted in going out. If he didn't land face down in a bog first.

"Hand me my socks." He pushed the blankets off.

The glaze of fever shone in his eyes. Perspiration fused his hair to his forehead. "I'm better." Toomas struggled to sit up but collapsed. "I'm getting dressed." One hand fumbled over the bedside.

Madli snatched his socks away. "The Nazis aren't coming today. You can rest."

Toomas made a weak gesture which wouldn't have maimed a fly. "They're counting on me. Most men are helping with the grain threshing so there's barely anyone left."

"Yes, yes." Madli yanked the covers over him. "You're indispensable and you're as weak as a newborn kitten." She muttered the last part.

A congested snore replied.

Madli placed the shoes and socks on the floor.

"Peeter, bring him water while I'm at the farm," Madli said. "I won't be long."

When Madli returned in late afternoon, Toomas was gone. As was Peeter.

"He can't be better," she muttered. "Where would he go?" There had been no sign of him as she walked through the camp. She placed the bottle of vodka Grandpa gave her beside the bed. Tonight she'd try another folk remedy — vodka socks.

Moments later, Toomas stumbled in and flung himself onto the bed.

"What are you doing?" Madli asked, furious as Toomas crawled under the blankets without taking his boots off. She tore the covers away and tugged off his muddy boots. "You're sick."

"I'm not sick," Toomas mumbled.

"Where did you go?" Madli's hand touched his burning forehead. "You'll make yourself sicker. Then what?"

Madli splashed water and vodka into a large bowl, threw his socks in, wrung out the liquid, and tugged them onto his feet.

"Hey!" Toomas's eyes flew open. "Those are cold."

Served him right for going out. "They'll warm up on your feet," Madli said with false hope. "Guaranteed to help your circulation and ease your congestion." She pulled a pair of thick wool socks on top of his wet ones.

"Good, because it's happening tomorrow." The lantern cast a wan light, making the hollows in Toomas's face black. Anticipation lit up his flushed face. "The Nazis land in Emmaste tomorrow."

CHAPTER TWENTY-THREE

Tomorrow. An ordinary word laced with extraordinary expectations.

If Toomas spent hours in the wet and cold, he'd develop pneumonia.

A sure death for him.

Another devastating loss for her.

Short of tying him to the bed, she couldn't prevent him from going.

"Perhaps the fever will break," Madli said, her voice flat. She tucked his blanket snugly around him. Tomorrow. Only hours away.

Toomas nodded. "Before dawn, I'll meet Jaan and the men." His eyelids fluttered. "The Soviets don't suspect anything." His words slurred at the end of the sentence. The outing had sapped his strength.

She was left with the faint hope that the vodka socks would work their magic.

For the want of a nail, the shoe was lost. For the want of a shoe, the horse was lost. A common fever threatened the success of the Nazi landing on Hiiumaa.

Madli sat down on her bed and stared at Toomas in the murky light. Like a ticking clock, each snore brought them closer to the morning. Every few minutes she would get up, walk over, touch his forehead, only to reaffirm the fact he was sick. Very sick. No amount of vodka socks or boiled milk with onions would restore Toomas to a healthy, strong young man capable of guiding the Nazis from their landing on the beach to the road.

Madli tucked Peeter into bed and snuffed out the lantern.

If Toomas couldn't go, who would?

So many had suffered. Thousands deported. Papa imprisoned in a cold Soviet jail. Kalju in a godforsaken part of Russia on the orders of the Soviet army. Mama had no idea where her family was. Did she imagine everyone gone? Dead? Buried?

A sob escaped. She couldn't risk losing Toomas. Over the last three months there had been moments of magic in hell. She'd lied to Papa about the lack of romance. On days when there was little hope of a future, all that existed was the present. Toomas had saved her life; now she had to save his.

Madli remembered standing with Papa in the cool spring breeze on top of the Eiffel Tower. His chocolate brown eyes sparkled as brightly as the lights of Paris below. The wind blew away his words as he pointed toward Montmartre, their destination the following day. Madli wore a crisp new linen dress, stiff and scratchy, cinched with a thin red leather belt around her waist. Papa's firm hand in hers and a stomach full of *pain au choc*. Hitler was on the verge of invading Poland. France would fall a year later to the Nazis. Soon thereafter, Jews would lose all their rights.

Within hours, the same Nazis were poised to liberate Estonia from the Soviets. Her emotions swirled like a kaleidoscope. And, like a kaleidoscope, there was no definitive viewpoint, only myriad options.

For the want of a horse the rider was lost. For the want of a rider the battle was lost.

Hot tears slid down her cheeks. Kalju may be dead. And Papa. In the dark, she shook her head to clear it. Morning would come, Toomas would be sick, and the Nazis would land. The only question was whether they would defeat the Soviets.

Rage boiled inside her.

Hadn't enough people died?

If she could help the Nazis, Papa could be freed, Kalju may come home, and Valter would be powerless. And Toomas wouldn't risk death.

Never mind the long history of dislike, even hatred, toward the German manor lords for hundreds of years of serfdom. Papa's disgust went into the back closet of her mind.

Madli had lived under the Soviet occupation for over a year and hadn't converted to Communism. Supporting the Nazis was similar. She wouldn't convert to their ideology.

Judenfrei.

Temporary. The Nazis would pass through, remove the Soviets, and move on to more important battles. The Nazis wouldn't want to stay in Estonia. What kind of advantage would a small corner of eastern Europe grant them?

The paths, roads, and trails were as familiar to Madli as the roads in Tallinn. If anyone knew the roads as well as Toomas, it was Madli. She'd played on every path throughout her life, every trail and road.

For the want of a battle, the kingdom was lost.

For the want of a guide, the Nazis were lost. For the want of the Nazis, Hiiumaa was lost.

No one would expect her to go in his place.

No one would expect her to aid the Nazis.

No one would imagine she could do such a thing.

Choices.

Like vanilla or chocolate.

Like freedom or integrity.

Freedom or the disappointment of her father. The guilt of perpetuating an ideology supporting the extermination of Jews and the creation of a master Aryan race.

Freedom or the integrity of one's convictions.

"Oma silm on kuningas."

Trust what you see yourself.

CHAPTER TWENTY-FOUR

A scuffling in the dark roused Madli. "Toomas?"

"Quiet." His normally smooth voice gurgled with congestion. "Don't wake Peeter."

"What are you doing?" Madli groped for the matches and lit the lantern. Toomas sat at the edge of his bed, hunched over like an old man.

"It's time to go." A cough punctuated his sentence.

"Where are you going?" Madli slid over beside him. Heat radiated toward her. His fever raged.

A shoe rested in his hand. He picked open the laces.

Madli snatched the shoe out of his hand, opened the tarp, and tossed the shoe into the forest. It landed with a thump.

"What did you do?" Anger shaded his voice. "I need that shoe." A frenzy of coughing followed and left him gasping for air.

"You must rest," Madli said. "Lie down." She shoved him onto his back.

His hands flailed in a half-hearted gesture.

"Peeter will find it later." Dawn was hours away. It wouldn't be light until eight o'clock this time of year. She'd be back by then. Madli pulled the covers up to Toomas's chin. "I'm going." The words slipped out without hesitation. Introspection was over. There was no time to waste.

His mouth gaped.

Madli grinned. "You look like a fish out of water." She tugged a pair of Toomas's pants onto her legs, followed by a sweater, warm wool jacket, and hat. A flashlight went into the pocket. Her hair stuck out under the hat. She tucked the offending strands under the wool cap. Madli peered into the small mirror. Better. Despite the shadows she observed the determination in her jawline, the clear focus in her eyes and the confident tilt of her head. Schoolgirl? What schoolgirl? The doubts in her mind faded. Helping the Nazis was the right thing to do. Her face told her so.

Madli tucked Peeter's wool mittens into her belt. Magic mittens. She needed magic today.

Toomas's hot hand grasped hers. "Be careful," he said weakly.

"I wouldn't do it for anyone else." Madli squeezed his hand. "Just for you."

"Don't do it for me," Toomas said. "Do it for yourself. And your country."

"I remember everything you talked about." At the time, she'd listened to Toomas's strategy with half an ear. Last night, however, she'd replayed the conversations in her head and was pleased with how much she remembered. "I'll direct them to the road and be back before breakfast." Madli kissed his forehead. "If anything happens to me ..."

"It won't," Toomas said. "It can't." He released her hand. "*Mine Jumalaga*. Don't forget the rifle. Remember to take up the slack on the trigger."

Madli pulled aside the tarp and stepped outside. Her eyes bored into the blackness as the cold air charged her lungs. The drone of a plane triggered a chill down her spine. No time for second thoughts, only time for action.

The last quarter of the moon cast its wan light toward the earth. She shuffled along the path, guided by a small pocket light. At the edge of the camp, Jaan and the men waited.

"Come on, Toomas," Jaan said. "Let's go."

Madli squared her shoulders, rifle dangling by her side, as she strode toward the men. The deception bolstered her confidence. She grunted a greeting and kept her head down.

"*Jõudu sulle*," Jaan saluted as they parted ways. The men set off in various directions to meet the Nazi troops at pre-assigned locations.

Strength, fortitude, bravery. Madli would need them all.

Luck wouldn't hurt either. Grandpa's words returned to her. *For us, woods are a sanctuary*. It was true. The darkness and foliage concealed and protected her. She tugged on her mittens.

She picked her way down the path toward the beach with eyes open wide, straining for traces of light. One icy foot in front of the other. The only sounds were her crisp steps and ragged breathing.

Philosophical musings be damned.

Madli stopped at the edge of the woods. A thick cloak of silence covered her.

Through the trees, the black sea glinted. An empty, glistening shoreline, dotted with rocks and boulders. The lengthy shallow beach eased into bog and forest. The walk from the sea to safety would be interminable.

The faint whirr of motorboats droned in the distance. The arrival of the hornet's nest.

Madli's heart thumped. Blood whooshed through her head and threatened to drown out the motors. She braced against a tree to calm down. Deep breaths of Baltic Sea air filled her lungs. Seabirds, salt, and the smell of winter.

Tiny shapes on the dark sea crawled closer to land. As the boats approached, the motors cut out and were tugged from the water. Gentle waves lapped the rocks. The water would be just shy of ice.

The spots on the sea divided into many. The Nazis hopped out of their motorboats and into the water. Shadows walked the open stretch. Gentle splashes and muttered curses travelled through the early morning calm as men stumbled over the rocks.

She wiggled her fingers for warmth inside the mittens.

Madli dreaded a volley of bullets, the staccato of gunfire from the forest where Soviet soldiers might hide. But all was quiet.

Madli stepped from the shelter of the trees to meet the soldiers. With each step, she lifted her foot out of the boggy land. Impossible to run on this kind of terrain. Impossible to hide on the open beach. Heat suffused her body. She tore open the top buttons of her jacket.

One foot in front of the other. No going back. The rifle butted her side.

Darkness couldn't conceal the broad shoulders of young men and the confident steps of conquerors. She did a quick count. Forty or so.

A tall silhouette approached her, the bottom half of his soaked uniform moulded to his body. His teeth chattered. He clenched his jaw before he spoke into his radio. *"Wir sind in Hiiumaa gelandet."*

"Guten Morgen," Madli said, surprised her words came out

steady and slow. *"Kommen sie auf diese wiese."* Shifting her weight from one foot to the other, she itched to get off the beach and into the shelter of the forest.

"Danke," Radio Man said.

Thank you. Words she hadn't heard from a soldier. With a hand signal and a quick command to his troops, he indicated they were set to follow her toward the road.

The motorboats faded into the distance. It wouldn't take long for the Nazis to fetch more men from Saaremaa Island. The distance from Hiiumaa was less than sixty kilometres.

In the shelter of the forest, Madli's shoulders were stiff blocks. The chill of the morning cut through her clothes. Clumsy frozen fingers buttoned up her jacket.

With the men at her heels, she picked up her pace. The rhythmic march of boots behind her was surprisingly comforting. Madli matched their tempo. Left, right, left, right, left, right, left. One frozen foot in front of the other. Quicker this time. Back along the path.

By the time they arrived at the main road, Madli was surprised to notice weak light filtering through the trees. She had no sense of time.

Radio Man pulled out a map and flashlight from his bag. *"Wo sind wir?"*

Madli stepped close enough to smell the sweat and the sea on his clothes. She snuck a quick peek at Radio Man. Though his uniform was half soaked, it was clean and well fitting. The part in his hair made a sharp line on the side of his head. Full lips and high cheekbones gave him the appearance of a Viking.

He caught her glance, narrowed his gaze to examine her closely.

A blush crept up her face, its heat welcome in the chill of the morning. He had realized she was a girl.

"*Mädchen*," he said in surprise. "*Du bist ein Mädchen.*"

"*Ja.*" Madli fingered the ends of her hair under the hat.

She found their location on the map and pointed out the way toward Nurste. Easy since there was only one road.

"*Vielen Dank, Fräulein.*" Radio Man snapped a salute in her direction, then a smile that wasn't the least bit military.

Madli's lips twitched in response. Horrified, her hand flew to her mouth to hide the smile. She'd never flirt with a Nazi but the relief of fulfilling her role in the mission made her giddy.

Radio Man spun on his heel, issued a couple of sharp commands and continued with his troops down the road. A dark mass of young men prepared to battle for Hiiumaa, perhaps to be wounded, to die. Sadness washed over her. Was Kalju walking down a dark road to fight the brothers or cousins of those Nazi men?

Kinder, kirche, und kuchen. And Christmas. They'd finally have Christmas again. A tree with lights and real presents, with pork and *verivorstid* and *kringel.* She jogged through the dimness of the forest. Maybe a new dress. Madli ran faster and faster back to Toomas and Peeter.

Oh, God. It was over. The Nazis would make fast work of the Red Army.

The squeal of a bomb brought her to a halt. The impact shuddered through Madli's legs.

Close.

Another bomb squealed. The ground rumbled in protest. Too close.

Close to Grandpa's farm.

Close to Toomas's farm.

Close to the manuscript.

Bomb after bomb crashed to the earth.

Oh, God.

Madli ran. Toward Toomas's farm. Toward Papa's manuscript.

⬧

Madli crashed through the woods. A burn spread through her chest and down her legs as she navigated over branches and around trees. The rifle drummed on her left leg. She willed the bombs to stay away from Toomas's old threshing barn where the papers lay nestled in the oven ashes.

Madli burst into the clearing, panting like a racehorse.

The morning sun dappled the cottage orange. Bent over, hands on her knees, her breathing slowed down. She tore off her mittens, tucked them into her pockets, and ripped open her jacket to cool down.

Bombs squealed to the ground as Madli walked toward the house.

The heavy oak door creaked as she shoved it open. Stepped over the threshold.

Stopped. Her legs anchored to the floor.

Flickering light from a lantern beside the bed drew her eye. Someone was inside.

Fear flooded her. Tensed her legs. Parched her mouth.

Madli hoisted the rifle to her shoulder. Took aim. Shooting wasn't the plan. She needed time to think.

"*Kurat!*" A man scrambled off the bench with hands in the air. He was dressed in simple clothes, a wool jacket and dark trousers. Not a soldier.

A familiar depth in his voice caused the hair on the back of her neck to prickle.

Valter?

Sensation emptied from her fingers. Madli tightened her grip on the trigger. Took up the slack. Took a deep breath.

It could be a farmer seeking refuge. It could be a young man from a neighbouring village.

Madli relaxed her finger.

She squinted. The man hadn't moved. Not an inch. He'd seen her finger on the trigger. Smart.

Same height as Valter. Same dark hair. Thinner. She tried to convince herself it wasn't him.

Her gut churned. It knew better.

What was he doing in the barn? Her eyes darted to the corners of the room. Anyone else?

"Don't hurt me." His voice cracked. "I'm an Estonian, running from the Nazis." He hesitated. "And the Soviets."

You're also a liar.

"I won't hurt you." His voice smoothed into persuasion. A vein protruded on his forehead.

Valter didn't recognize her.

Madli stepped toward him.

Hollows formed craters in his cheeks. His hair, once thick, lay limp. "Please." He waved his hands in front of him.

The rank odour of old sweat hit her nostrils. The smell of a Soviet soldier.

Madli clutched the rifle in front of her face so he wouldn't notice her eyes. "Who are you?" She forced her voice into a deep growl.

A glance around the barn told her he'd been there for a while. A rifle leaned on the wall. A rumpled grey blanket lay on the bed. A plate with crumbs of black bread sat on the table.

"Sit down." Madli waved her rifle at the bed in the corner of the room. There'd be less chance of him attacking her.

Valter moved toward her.

Madli stepped back. A mistake. A sign of weakness.

Valter lunged at her.

Madli's finger tightened. Squeezed.

Before she could pull the trigger, the barrel smacked the side of her head. Hot pain stabbed through her skull. The rifle clattered to the floor.

Madli crashed to the ground on all fours.

Kurat. Her teeth jabbed into her lip. This was not the time for tears. Short shallow breaths helped her ignore the hurt.

Valter pounced on the rifle. "Get up," he commanded harshly.

Madli glanced sideways. Two rifle barrels levelled at her. She blinked. There was only one. Valter's stance told her he wouldn't hesitate to shoot. Why hadn't she pulled the trigger? Kalju never had a second chance.

Warm tears coated her hands. Disobedience would earn her a shot in the head. She had to reveal her identity.

"Get up," Valter growled.

"You wouldn't shoot me." Madli scrambled to her feet. Satisfaction at his gaping mouth and confused eyes kept her knees from crumpling. Gingerly, she touched the side of her throbbing head.

The rifle dipped. "Madli," Valter whispered.

"I thought you were with the Soviets," Madli said. White stars sparked in front of her eyes. She clutched the table. Sat down hard on the bench. The stars faded.

A look flickered over his face. Shame? Guilt? Annoyance at being caught?

"I escaped," Valter said.

"You're on the wrong side," Madli taunted him. "Again."

Valter sat down across the table from her, one hand around the rifle barrel. "Why are you here?" His nails were grimy, thick with black.

"I was going to the farm." Her breath feathered upward in the chill. She had no intention of telling him about Papa's manuscript. The oven would be unused since smoke would be a target for planes.

Valter shook his head.

"You're a coward," Madli snarled, her voice ice. It was the wrong thing to say, but she couldn't help it. "You desert the Soviets to protect yourself. You hide here. Did you ever consider Grandpa and Nana, the people who raised you, provided you a home and family?" Saliva gathered in her mouth. Her lips pursed to spit at him.

"They hate me because I joined the Soviets." Valter focused on a spot on the window beside her.

He couldn't meet her eyes. Madli swallowed. "I never told them. I couldn't."

Valter's eyes widened. A flicker of gratitude. "Thank you. I don't deserve that."

"It wasn't for you." That was true.

"There's nothing here." Valter glanced around. "I've been here for days." He had the grace to look guilty. "You wouldn't come here unless there was a reason. What are you searching for?"

Madli shrugged one shoulder. "I noticed the light and wondered who was here."

Another bomb rattled the window.

"You happened to be walking in the woods?" His eyes searched the room. "In the middle of a battle. With bombs falling. It must be important."

Claustrophobia tightened her throat. Madli hated his face, his voice, everything about him. A shy farm boy turned traitor. His choice, his fate.

Madli thrust her hands into her trouser pockets. She had to leave. The manuscript could be retrieved another day. A weird satisfaction at his confusion gave her a trace of bravado. "Can I have my rifle? I'm leaving." She gambled he still had enough fondness for her not to shoot. "They're waiting for me at the farm."

Valter shook his head. "How can I be certain you won't shoot me?"

Madli's finger crooked along an imaginary trigger. "Because I had the chance." Sarah's voice from months ago whispered in her ear. *You can catch more flies with honey than vinegar.* The game needed to be played. Her lips forced a smile. A tiny one. "I couldn't." His affection for her was the only weapon she had.

She compelled her legs to stand. "Keep the rifle. I'm leaving. You should leave also. The woods are crawling with Nazis." A bit of friendly advice wouldn't hurt.

Valter stood up, lifted the rifle.

He was going to shoot her.

Valter's hand reached for the bolt. He snapped it back and forth.

The screaming in her head never reached her mouth.

A bullet fell out of the gun and hit the floor with a dull thud. He repeated the action four more times. "Here."

"What?" The scream faded.

"Take it." Valter held out the rifle. "Not that I don't trust you."

Relief flooded her. Sensation returned to her fingers, her toes, her legs. Madli's hand gripped the cold steel of the barrel.

Valter placed a clammy hand over hers. "Don't hate me." Apology flooded his brown eyes.

Without a backward glance, Madli marched out of the threshing barn and across the dew-wet grass. The imprint of his damp hand haunted her skin. She rubbed her hand against the scratchy wool jacket.

A bomb pounded into the ground. Her body trembled like gelatin.

A coward would shoot her in the back. It took every ounce of strength to resist looking over her shoulder. Madli focused on the rough bark of a pine tree.

Six steps to go.

Five. Four. She lengthened her stride. Two. One.

Inside the protection of the trees, Madli fingered the extra bullets in her pocket as she ducked behind the pine.

❖

How much anger would she need to kill Valter?

Was she a fool for not pulling the trigger or a hero for not giving in to hate? Had she given Valter carte blanche to continue terror and killing?

Who was the coward?

Dodging from tree to tree, she hiked toward Grandpa's farm. Her head pounded from the blow of the rifle. A mittened hand patted her temple. Pain pierced her teeth.

The last person she had expected to see was Valter. Madli choked on the cold morning air. It slid down her into lungs, but she couldn't get enough oxygen. Shooting him was wishful thinking. That battle would be fought by someone else.

Bomb after bomb whistled through the air. The ground quaked as Madli approached Grandpa and Nana's farm. If only a blast would flatten the threshing barn. That would take care of things. Never mind the manuscript. It was paper. It didn't represent the truth or Papa any more than her helping the Nazis meant she supported their ideology. Papa would be proud of her with or without the manuscript. That was the truth.

Maybe.

The aching hurt in her skull prevented her from thinking any more.

❖

At the farm, a dozen Nazi soldiers stood on the porch. Young men with pink cheeks from the morning chill. In the crisp light, their drab uniforms contrasted with the pleasant yellow of the house. The final crumbs of a loaf of bread disappeared into one soldier's mouth. He wiped it clean with his sleeve and assembled his pack.

Nana yanked out the wooden poles used to stake the open areas. A pile lay by the fence.

"Nana!" Madli rushed over.

Nana gathered her in a bony hug. Her grandmother appeared all thinness and fragility, but the strength of her arms crushed the breath from Madli.

"What happened here?" Nana stroked Madli's cheek.

Madli's hand touched the soreness where the rifle had whacked her. "I ran into a tree branch." This wasn't the time to tell Nana she'd escorted the Nazi army through the forest and confronted Valter.

"Look," Nana said. She slid out of the embrace, but kept one arm around Madli's waist.

Grandpa stood by the flagpole and hoisted the Estonian flag. Halfway up the pole, the flag fluttered in the breeze, as if to test its strength, then snapped to its full size at the top. The words of the national anthem, locked inside for over a year, drifted out of Madli's mouth in a whisper. "*Mu isamaa, mu õnn ja room, kui kaunis oled sa.*" She glanced over her shoulder, half expecting Soviet soldiers to jump out of the forest, rifles raised in protest. Only days ago, in a village near Valga, a boy Peeter's age had his fingers broken after his family had raised the flag on their farm. The furious soldiers had shot the father, then twisted the boy's fingers until they broke.

"The colours of the flag are symbolic." Grandpa lectured the soldiers in German. His finger traced an arc to the sky. "Blue is for the colour of our Baltic sky." He bent down and let the soil cascade through his fingers. "Black is for the fertile soil." He stood up and placed a hand over his heart. "And white is for the purity of our hearts."

The soldiers nodded. One shook Grandpa's hand. "*Danke*."

His chin firm, Grandpa turned to face the flag.

The flag blurred into a prism of blue, black, and white. Madli blinked back tears.

The Nazi soldiers hoisted their packs and walked toward the road.

Madli ran after them. "*Bitte!*"

The commander stopped. "*Fraulein?*"

Her breath caught in her throat. The words wouldn't come out. What good would it do?

The commander waited patiently, as if he had all morning to watch a girl gape like a baby bird waiting for a worm.

"There's a man, a Soviet soldier, hiding in a barn over in the next farm." Madli described the location of the barn. As the words left her, so did the lump in her stomach.

The commander nodded. "If he's there, we'll deal with him."

Deal with him. Good.

⚜

As Madli hurried back to the camp, the lump returned to her stomach. It sat heavy until it the weight of it made her sink to the ground. On her hands and knees, cold damp seeped through her pants and chilled her fingers. How could she be so cruel? Her impulsiveness could cost Valter his life.

Foreign feelings of retribution and revenge shamed her.

What had this war caused her to do?

Her breath caught.

Regret blasted through her. Oh, God forgive her.

Madli bent over and lay her forehead on the frosty ground. The solid earth and the smell of life infused her with strength. She gathered icy crumbs of dirt and let them trickle between her numb fingers.

As she lay there, a shell began to form around the memory of her betrayal. Layer by layer, her justifications for divulging Valter's location formed a coating substantial enough that she could lift her head. Look into her conscience. Forgive herself enough.

This secret would stay locked inside her. No one would ever find out.

❖

Madli tore open the tarp to their shelter at the Forest Brothers' camp. "The Nazis are here," she announced, breathless. "They're on their way up the coast toward Nurste." She bounced on the bed beside Toomas.

Toomas squeezed her hand. "*Hästi tehtud.*" His voice barely carried.

The pride in his eyes sparked a blush to creep into her cheeks.

Madli laid a hand on his forehead. Cooler. She was certain. Relief flooded her. "Here, drink this water." She held a cup to his lips.

His hot hand grasped hers. "Happy birthday." A weak grin crossed his lips. "A hell of a way to turn sixteen."

Madli's smile spread from ear to ear. "Yes." She lay down beside him, her head on his chest. "Freedom is the best present."

Sunday, October 12, 1941

Kallis Papa,

Helping the Nazis may have been the wrong thing to do, but

I did it for the right reasons. To get rid of the Soviets and to stop the killing, even a little.

As I write this, the bombs drop like rain around us. I can't sleep.

The Nazis landed on the beach at Emmaste, Külaküla, and Harju küla this morning. By nightfall, Emmaste was liberated. The soldiers are making their way up the coast. The island will be free within days.

Freedom on my sixteenth birthday. When you get home, I'll bake a kringel and we'll celebrate. Palju õnne sünnipäevaks!

Monday, October 13, 1941

Kallis Papa,

One final Soviet killing spree. The bastards. The Soviet soldiers killed thirteen innocent people in Nurste today. They tossed the bodies into the dry river bed of Laartse. One woman escaped. She pleaded and begged with the Soviet soldier. Amazingly, he let her go. If only the other thirteen had been so lucky.

PART THREE